No One
is
Looking
at
You

JAMES MAGRUDER

Rattling Good Yarns Press
33490 Date Palm Drive 3065
Cathedral City CA 92235
USA
www.rattlinggoodyarns.com

Cover Photograph © Carla Zackson

Library of Congress Control Number: 2025940492
ISBN: 978-1-955826-88-4

First Edition

PRIOR PUBLICATION ACKNOWLEDGMENTS

Several of these stories were previously published in slightly different form as follows:

"Cufflinks" in *StoryQuarterly*

"Faculties" in *The Idaho Review*

"Tree Surgeon" and "Hoo-Whee" in *The Hopkins Review*

"Milestone" in *Baltimore City Paper*

"Orality" in *Welter*

"Nightstand" in *AU*

"Worth Our Breath," a chapbook in letterpress. The Literary House Press

Also by James Magruder

Fiction

Sugarless

Let Me See It

Love Slaves of Helen Hadley Hall

Vamp Until Ready

Theater

Three French Comedies

The Play's the Thing: Fifty Years of Yale Repertory Theatre (1966-2016

Contents

Part One
Origin Stories

"Joe, macht die Musik von damals nach."
~*Der Bilbao-Song*

Milestone

It was early October, six weeks since his freshman year had started, and Gordon Trax had no friends to present to his father, who was coming up for his eighteenth birthday and a National Dairy Board Conference in Syracuse. "Biff, Scooter, Seb and I got plowed at the Big Game last weekend" was the kind of shit Gordon's brother, Kennie, used to sling over the wires from his frat at UVA, the kind of shit to send their father out to the driveway basketball hoop to play horse with their stepbrothers. Gordon felt that news from his vicinity had always sent Ted Trax's hand checking for his half-glasses in his vest pocket.

Gordon couldn't conjure any Scooters to pal with for the visit, and worse, he had used up valuable conversation over the phone.

"It took me the longest time, Daddy, to figure out the difference between an elastic and an inelastic good," said Gordon. "Demand constant with price fluctuations. I had to graph it out." This sounded idiotic to his own ears, but he crashed on nevertheless. "So, I would guess that milk, being a staple, would have an inelastic demand."

Ted Trax caught the hook. "You'd be surprised, son."

"What?"

"How much milk we have to destroy."

"Why is that, sir?"

"The government makes us dump it. Dairy farmers grow too much. People don't drink more milk just because it costs less. Think about it."

"But it's milk. How can you destroy milk?" Gordon hated to see even half a glass go down the drain, but, unfortunately, his sympathy stopped their dialogue in microeconomic theory.

"You need money?"

"No."

"What about your birthday?"

"No."

Ted laughed and said he'd see him at the crack of dawn on Saturday.

After hanging up, Gordon looked at his Latin reader until a knock at the door reminded him that he did have one friend. Coming in with a deck of cards, Spencer Mercer hissed that his roommate, Cy Aranow, had imported DeeDee Shrader over for more giggling lascivities. Gordon could hear Joni Mitchell warming DeeDee up through the cinderblock wall that separated their rooms.

Spencer dealt a three-thousandth hand of gin rummy, his long fingers moving like crabs over the cards. The Cornell Hotel School could not have produced a more dissimilar twosome than squat, gummy Cy Aranow and ruddy, freakishly tall, horn-billed Spencer Mercer, who, being from Bermuda, could not appreciate his likeness to Ichabod Crane. Spencer's fidelity to cards discharged Gordon from the roll call of the complete untouchables. They played facing Gordon's open door, and turned up their volume when others walked by, a desperate ruse they chose not to acknowledge to one another.

Spencer was also Gordon's first experience in gauging how rich people might turn out to be. After a week of rummy and cultural exchange, he asked him whether the Mercers belonged to the ruling class of Bermuda.

"The Queen rules Bermuda, silly."

"But I'll bet you help," said Gordon, not intending to be rude.

"Dads is in the government. Bermuda doesn't need much looking after, actually."

"Have you any servants?"

"Excuse me?"

Gordon rephrased. "Have you many servants?"

"As many as are needed to keep the properties up."

"That many," nodded Gordon.

No one else was awake when Gordon, looking through the window at the far end of the corridor, spotted his father's Buick pulling up. They would buy a Cornell bumper sticker, maybe a shot glass, but then there would be hours of what?

Ted Trax stepped out of the car, picked once, twice, at the right side of his crotch—a post-drive gesture of his—and Gordon rushed down the stairs. The fifty-dollar birthday transaction happened during their embrace in the parking lot. The check poked out of Gordon's shirt pocket all day. He couldn't think of a subtle way to remove it.

"I don't know the place very well, sir."

His father briefly cupped the back of Gordon's head in his hand. "Don't get anxious, Gord-o."

That his father did have a clue kept him from clutching. Gordon let him talk as they toured Cornell in an early autumn chill. He talked about the new house he was going to build, a house big enough to hold the steps, the halfs, Kennie, and Gordon, who visualized him as the chimney holding up its center.

At the campus store, his father bought a pile of sweatshirts, a set of brandy snifters with the school crest, and when Gordon let it drop that he had played nine holes of golf with "this guy from Bermuda"—never again would Spencer sound so rugged—he pressed a pair of golf shoes on him with such vigor that Gordon felt the cleats on his chest. He stopped him at the pitching wedge.

Ted Trax felt it his duty to buy his son a drink on his eighteenth birthday. Muggsy's in Collegetown was the first place they spotted that served at lunch. Gordon couldn't pretend he'd been there, and let his father order. He kept up his end by having one beer to Ted's every two. When Ted began to overdo it with the waitress, who looked no older than a graduate student, Gordon was unable to hide his embarrassment.

Ted, to his credit, made the connection. "Son," he said abruptly, "let me tell you about Lily Anne."

For coming of age in New York State, Gordon was getting fresh facts of life.

"I know about Lily Anne."

"You know your mother's version of Lily Anne."

Gordon began watching a parade of streamers, pennants, and plaid coats heading for the Cornell v. Colgate football game. He should have thought about getting them tickets.

"You met Lily Anne once."

"I never did, no sir."

"But you did, Gord-o. Do you remember going to a restaurant called the Ram, up in Richmond?" Ted was counting on Gordon's unearthly sense of recall. "I drove you and Kennie up there one visitation weekend."

"I was only ten," Gordon said.

"If you remember you were ten, then you remember."

It felt unusual to have his father feeding him cues.

"The bathrooms said Rams and Ewes"—here Gordon stopped. "She must have brought you your scotch."

"She served food too, Gordon," said Ted, irritated by the cocktail waitress dig.

Gordon shrugged. "It came late. I used to take off for the john when I got tired of waiting for my food. I must have actually had to pee at the Ram, because when I got back, you told me to wait until I got into the bathroom to unzip. Did Lily Anne see me undo my fly in front of everybody?"

His father was now giving Gordon a look like having their dicks hang out was an endearing family trait. "She did point it out."

"Great with kids, huh?"

"She had her own. She wanted to meet mine."

"You showed Mom their report cards."

"I—shit son, that was a mistake. Drink up."

Their subsequent pause was agonizingly long, the two of them swiping looks and making little man noises after chugs, a pause so long that for an instant Gordon was worried his father was going to grab his hand and hold it. He sometimes did that on long car rides when conversation dried up. Finally, Ted half-laughed himself into wondering why Gordon never asked him any questions.

Instead of asking if he had wanted to go to the football game, Gordon said, "Did Lily Anne say anything else about me?"

"She talked to you. You had a conversation. You charmed her."

"That I don't remember."

"I didn't marry Lily Anne, son." He was getting pissed again, pissed on top of being half-pissed from the beers.

"Then why are we talking about her?"

"She's having a hysterectomy next month."

After his father drove off, with a kiss and another twenty to his shirt pocket, Gordon sat at his desk chair and laced his golf cleats, amazed at how things could play out. Ted Trax hadn't felt the need to explain the why or the what or the how of Lily Anne, the cocktail waitress who tore their family up, but this matter of *duration* puzzled Gordon. How could they still possibly be in touch? Here he had sired out of two women, confused his wives when in his cups, and decided that the impending loss of her uterus was just cause for discussing his old mistress for the first time with his second son. Gordon tried to shrug off this strange mantle dropped on his shoulders, but the beer buzz, plus a milestone passed, depressed him.

He ignored Spencer's gin rummy knock and felt homicidal when reading the birthday card slid under his door. He would either have to kill Spencer for being his changeling in pathos, or go mad. At dinner he ate three pieces of cake, but then, around nine, when he heard a knot of hallmates gather cross-legged outside their doors as they did most nights, instead of staring into a future of solitary intellectual overcompensation, he marched out and began to entertain the troops. After he'd got them laughing, he got them to talk about themselves, and made many a smart-ass quip. He sang jingles, jogged their memories about defunct game shows, crappy hit songs of yesteryear, Saturday cartoons, double-play combinations, asked them about which classes they were taking, talked in funny voices, overdid his Virginia drawl for effect, practiced his golf swing, talked smut hellbent for slick, asked out loud for drugs and booze, swapped S.A.T. scores, tap-danced to the window at the end of the hall and serenaded some hapless coed with the theme song from The Mary Tyler Moore Show. All that he did, he did for at least two hours, only wishing he could have snake-charmed them to sleep in the hallway and watched to make sure his rubber cement had dried them all together.

The next morning, Gordon was dressed and ready when they were heading off for breakfast. In another two days, they'd knock on his door before attempting a meal. Two weeks after his birthday, he was their lieutenant.

Tree Surgeon

Difficult to believe, but once upon a time, diversity on college campuses was as much a question of geography as race or economic background. The College of Arts and Sciences at Cornell University had to pull at least one student from every state every year.

Kevin Crawley was Idaho 1978. His hometown, Wallace, didn't have a dirty bookstore, just cattle and sugar beets, and crosses along the highway for friends who had died of boredom and a need for speed. When Kevin started Cornell, he was needy for something else. During his first week in Ithaca, he bought an issue of *Blueboy* magazine in the Co-Op. He stowed it beneath his winter sweaters in the bottom of his travel trunk, the sort that doubled as a coffee table for books and bongs. After six weeks of talking to the hand with the magazine, Kevin wrote a facsimile of his first name inside a toilet stall in the basement bathroom of Willard Straight Hall, the student union, with the words "17-year old virgin wants to change all that," and his phone number.

For forty-eight hours, he stayed out of his suite in U-Hall 3 from fear, then forgot what he'd done, enough to be totally unnerved when a voice asked for Karl one afternoon.

"This is K-K-K—he."

(Kevin was a stutterer; his application essay had made skillful light of it, granting him admission to Stanford, the University of Chicago, Vanderbilt, and Tufts, as well as Cornell.)

"I read your message."

"Y-y-ye-es."

"Maybe we could get together, Karl. Are you cute?"

"S..s...s...some. Are you?"

He knew that sounded defensive. If he hadn't been a stutterer, Kevin might have majored in communications at the University of Idaho with the goal of becoming a newscaster. Instead, he grew up terse, righteous, over-achieving, and apt to be heard—and then taken—the wrong way.

"I'm twenty-six," the voice answered.

Kevin silently processed this alarming piece of news. He'd been planning for a less-than-virginal Big Red, Class of '79 or '80.

"Are you there, Karl?"

"My n-n-name is really Kuh-kuh-evin."

"Okay. I'm Jim"

He asked Jim where they should meet.

"Do you have a roommate, Kevin?"

"I have three," he replied, his voice cracking.

"How about we meet in the Willard Straight parking lot?"

"When?"

"7:45 tomorrow."

"Morning or evening?"

Kevin laughed. "You're funny."

"How will I know you, Jim?" When Kevin was able to manage a full sentence of one-syllable words at first strike, like this one, he risked sounding snide.

"I'm blond, and I've got a car."

Walking up Libe Slope, looking for leaves to scuff, Kevin repeated to himself that he was free not to step into Jim's car. When he spotted the man leaning against the door of an open blue Pinto, the first thing he decided was that he didn't look like one.

Jim Willits, with blond, wavy hair and a full mustache, greeted Kevin with, "I can tell right away you're not Jewish."

(That's enough stuttering.)

"I am a Catholic. From Idaho."

They exchanged a look under the streetlight, and Kevin sensed he'd be safe. Jim was a large man, solid and confident, not to mention twenty-six felt established in a major way. Although he was free not to, Kevin stepped into the Pinto.

Jim was a psychology grad student who was interning part-time in Trumansburg in a home for male juvenile offenders. Many were intellectually challenged, and the size of bears, and Jim sometimes had to restrain them. His hands dancing over his lap like a drunken sign interpreter, Kevin wondered whether undergraduates were a change of pace for Jim. He had no idea where they were driving, except in the woods, and where he was going to lose his virginity when Jim asked:

"What do you think you might like to do?"

Kevin was fidgeting so hard in the bucket seat, waiting for this segue, that he almost put his head through the roof when it came, knew what Jim meant. But everything was suddenly so *bald*. "What do you mean?" he replied, like some dopey pre-teen.

"I mean with me," Jim said in a low voice.

"Why are you asking me that?"

"I don't want to scare you. There are different things to do. I wanted to talk to you first and make sure you got to know who I was."

Kevin stammered out what interested him—basically, everything—and Jim listened, making comforting moves with his voice, face, and body. He didn't mention the stutter even when it took Kevin what felt like seven 'b's" and forty-eight "j's" to get through the word "blowjob."

They drove north, then parked just inside the gate of the Cornell Plantations. There were lights in the distance. Kevin listened for a bit but could identify no nighttime nature sounds, except the rushing of the falls over Beebe Lake. Jim leaned over and placed his index finger under Kevin's chin. "If you don't like anything that's happening, let me know, and we'll stop."

They began. Kevin made sure to keep his eyes open. Men *did* kiss. The issue of *Blueboy* had been mum on the subject; he was more anxious about foreplay issues than he was with the fact of actual sex. The car steamed up, and he was able to laugh when Jim reached over and traced a smiley face on the passenger window. Despite the chill, they took their amazing, fantastic trashiness out against a tree, Kevin only tensing up when he wasn't able to get a handful of Jim when he wanted it. The event had to be about both of them.

Back in the car, buttoning his shirt, Kevin apologized for taking such a long time *this* time. Jim missed, or ignored, the inflection.

"You were just tense, Kevin." Then, because molesting the willing would seem to have its own patter, Jim continued. "You're a natural."

This compliment should have been delivered as Kevin was closing the car door, but Jim miscalculated and still had two hundred yards to go, time enough to give Kevin three pieces of advice, two of which he committed to memory. (The third is lost to time.)

1) Never take it up the butt.
2) Don't fall in love with me.

Kevin wouldn't claim to have forgotten what had happened, but it wasn't until his chemistry lecture the next morning that circumstances permitted a recap. A granola girl walked into Goldwin Smith Hall wearing a "Please Don't Touch My Tuts" T-shirt. (The blockbuster "Treasures of Tutankhamun" show was currently touring the major art museums of America.) The sentiment, the two sarcophagi masks on the shirt, her long braid, plus the apple in her hand flushed out the night with Jim Willets in high relief.

Kevin discovered, with an itchy luxury, that he had joined something. The professor was lecturing on electron shells, the areas in which an electron and its partners on that level might be found: although one could never track them specifically, the electron might announce its position suddenly, like a firefly. In high school, Kevin would walk the nighttime streets of Wallace, Idaho, and wonder in which houses the neighbors were doing it. He knew that sex was happening all around him, but where exactly? Bedroom lights blinked off, lovers spent, out of reach, and there he'd be, three houses away, sniffing for it.

It turned out that sex did not necessarily reveal itself. Kevin could have leaped up from his seat in the lecture hall and witnessed: "I am now a sexual being. Anyone who wants to can smell my fingers," but he was already somewhere else in the electron shell. He had gotten past worrying who got it or not and could wave goodbye to Idaho Kevin guessing in the dark.

This subjective confrontation with quantum mechanics did not neglect the sensate. Kevin's time in the woods had yielded a quilled stomach that moved like his, a pair of eggs that felt like a roll of half-dollars, a solid frame that let him crawl on, legs that gripped, the feel of a mustache, and the full, pulpy, head to foot smack of male flesh.

He met up with Jim Willets a second time, after a demeaning will-he won't-he call? song-and dance by his telephone. Kevin spotted him going into Ives Hall. Encounter #2 was more of the same, with none of the preamble. Jim let Kevin spend the night with him in his apartment, with a view that looked over the gray pancake of the Collegetown IGA roof.

Kevin admired the spare way of his dresser top. Loose change, bookmarks, books of matches, cologne, comb. Jim lit a candle on his nightstand after the lights were out, but not before Kevin, shivering with heat, not cold, watched all of the big man undress. Alone, in a room, with a man, naked, for him. His face must have been working strangely because Kevin smiled, sat on the bed, and softly said, "Climb aboard."

Kevin did not fall in love for very long. Pride kept him from stalking Jim any further. A couple of weeks later, on the way to dinner at Willard Straight, he checked out their stall in the basement bathroom. Jim had scribbled "not anymore" next to "virgin" in Kevin's original message. Kevin flushed many shades of mortification over his meal that night. He was just one more emotionally challenged boy taken against a tree in the park. On December 6th, the Feast of St. Nicholas, when Kevin picked up the phone in his suite, and a med student named Sanjay told him that Jim Willets had said he was cute, and could they meet up for some, you know, *activity*, Kevin refused, then seriously considered paying a visit to the Psychology Department to meet with the Director of Graduate Studies.

Orality

Maggie Rand's undisciplined rage at her "prick father" had convinced Jason Packer that she needed someone sensitive to minister to her agenda. She was given to lengthy, feminist rhetorical tangents. All men were pricks, she'd insist, except for Jason, who spoke French *comme un ange,* and had nice broad *épaules* to boot.

The way she'd said she wished it had been her father, and not his, who had dropped dead gave him the idea to ask her for a date that December of his sophomore year. Since they hadn't any history besides French class freshman year, Maggie seemed an ideal choice for rehabbing his manhood. He could still see his roommate Gomez's eyes roll whenever he'd pick up the phone and use his French with Maggie. Gomez was seeing an Ag student Jason had secretly nicknamed Motogirl for her shapely body and the tangled, black helmet of her hair.

"What about Patrick McDermott?" Jason had asked Maggie a week after he had written Patrick a lengthy, unanswered declaration of love. "Is he a prick?"

Maggie had met Patrick just the once, but she knew what to say. "I know he's your friend, Jason, but don't you find him rather merchant class?"

"His father sells grocery scales."

"My point exactly."

Jason didn't always get Maggie's points. Before his death, his father had been a CFO for an apple juice company. Did an accountant outrank a salesman? Then, in supposed afterthought, Maggie added, "The Irish are particularly repressed. I would never date a man who wasn't oral."

Orality was a gauntlet Jason was ready to shoulder when he met Maggie outside Risley College in the winter moonlight. He'd picked an offbeat first date—an open sing of "The Messiah" at Risley, then and now the preferred residence of Cornell's cultural left, a Gothic Revival structure ideal for art fairs, human chess games, and group sex.

Stamping her feet in the cold, the tall and angular Maggie looked sophisticated in a violet beret. "Boy Meets Girl," Jason thought, as he grabbed both her gloves in his. As they walked the vaulted corridor to the dining hall, he asked Maggie what her favorite Christmas carol was.

"'Angels We Have Heard on High.'"

"Mine is 'The Little Drummer Boy.'"

"That's a sad one."

"Is it?" he said.

She laughed and squeezed his arm.

The prospect of singing *The Messiah* made even the Risley Trotskyites dapper and penitent. Beards were trimmed; hair was tamed, and not a pair of construction boots in sight. Jason felt free to get lost among the baritones, lift his voice, and watch Maggie across a nave hung with spruce and holly, equally lost among the sopranos, a little girl putting out cookies for Santa before the chords crashed and her father pricked up his marriage.

Pity is a bad rationale for sex, making a two-sided mercy fuck a weepy disaster. Maggie and Jason were so puling after the Handel and a post-concert cocoa at Noyes Pancake House, that they didn't make much progress. They nearly cracked their skulls together trying to be the first to demonstrate their orality. Maggie eventually called a time-out. It was embarrassing, but essential, she said, for their half-dressed selves to admit that they scarcely knew one another.

They tried to backtrack the next week. The idea would be to get to know each other well enough to support further "genitocentrism." (Maggie had a nonce word for everything.) They would extend a mutual invitation to share their fears and formations, disclose the information they would need to grow to trust one another, and lay the groundwork for a healthy and appropriately adult relationship.

That was the theory. In practice, it worked more like "Dial-a-Porn." Maggie would relate her sexual fantasies over the phone, and Jason would do his best to squint himself into her picture frame.

"I'm thinking about a tub full of raspberry Jell-O, solidifying all around my body," she said Tuesday night. "I have a thing for raspberries."

"They're a luxury good," he replied, at a loss. He was taking International Trade Theory that semester.

"And then when the Jell-O is set, and firm, and I'm trapped inside it, and...."

Jason made an effort. "And someone loosens you...?"

"And then I make love with my savior for *hours*, the heat of our bodies melting the Jell-O...."

"No," he interrupted, "the cool of the Jell-O keeps us from perspiring...." (Was he really saying this?)

"What's wrong with sweat, Jason?"

"Um. It smells bad?"

Sophisticated Maggie declared that funk was fun, so Jason apologized for the gaffe. Funk, male or female, had not been a positive in his upbringing.

"No, Jason, I apologize. If cleanliness is your thing, live and let live. I'm more European. Tell me one of your fantasies."

But he never did. Not with Gomez three feet away. Truthfully, Jason Packer hadn't permitted himself sexual fantasies. While his high school years had included a number of girls and boys with whom he had wanted to mate, he was too self-conscious about his husky frame and man boobs to picture himself ever doing the deed. Maggie mentioned several times that fat was a feminist issue, but whether that meant Jason was supposed to lose weight, or gain weight, under her supervision, he never found out. Best guess: she loved pithy sayings.

After the week of Jell-O—and tulip fields near a windmill in ruins— over the phone, Maggie chose their second date: a Law School Film Society screening of *Cries and Whispers*. This not five hours after a pap smear at Campus Health Services. With the dice now loaded for snake eyes, God alone would know whether they were mature enough *not* to have sex. Because Maggie had made it clear that trips to the gynecologist were devastatingly invasive, Jason upped the stakes by bringing her a long-stemmed red rose. There he waited, fifth in line for the Bergman at Uris Hall, forgetting that out of water, his gesture would wither. It delighted her, nonetheless.

The graphic intensity of *Cries and Whispers* ruled out an insouciant malted with fries after. They trudged to her room. Maggie's roommate, Alicia, was spending the weekend following the Grateful Dead with her boyfriend. Jason sat down on Maggie's single and waited while she put his rose in a Bryn Mawr coffee mug on her desk. All night long, he would clock the precarious tilt of its stem.

À propos of nothing, Maggie declared, as Jason was carefully pulling up her sweater, her horror of penetration. There was no gain in it for her. To keep things moving, Jason agreed to wait for however long it took. Far be it for him to displease her; he just didn't want to have to make Jell-O in a dorm kitchen at two o'clock in the morning.

Once they began, Jason found it helpful to forget about himself, and eventually, with luck, after he'd learned the nuances of when and where to kiss her, and how long, and with what amount of pressure, Maggie would forget about him, too.

He hoped she wouldn't notice that he wasn't fully present between her legs. He kept going, apologizing the only way he knew how for the brutish beefheads in her past, for guys like his brothers, frat boys who wouldn't feel they owed her anything, for Napoléon and Hitler and Nixon and Pol Pot, and her creepy Health Services OB-GYN, and that messed-up Swedish genius Ingmar Bergman.

After they had finished, Jason imagined that the rest of the baritone section felt sated, but he felt exhausted. He slunk home, duty ebbing away in each duck boot he pressed into the ground. The bleacher of men whom he'd needed to watch him through Maggie's window blinds could now pass through the stadium turnstile, go home to wake up wifey with their beer-swollen tongues, and leave him be. He had earned the right to dream about merchant class Patrick McDermott on his pillow.

Jason failed to notice Gomez's necktie strung around the doorknob to their room, the "Action Within" signal from the time of their grandfathers, and opened the door. No other verb than *plow* can describe the immoderate strides Gomez was marking into Motogirl, whose real name was Jill. She was arched under him, moaning, her luxurious hair sweeping the pillow. His hair hid much of his face, but Jason could just spot his roommate's teeth clenched in a smile. Against the sheets, Gomez was ruddy, Jill was alabaster, like a Renaissance painting, although canvases hung in museums couldn't capture the crashing music they made.

Jason slammed the door. Through the wall he heard them giggle. They were anything but ashamed. Waiting outside, removing his gloves, he recognized their abandon for what it was, and what it was, was *anointed*. Gomez and Jill were man and woman catching fire with each other in a Baroque visitation stoked by Vulcan's hammer. Maggie and Jason, on the other hand, had been a line drawing in a Catholic dating manual.

For the time being, there was nothing for him to do but tighten his shoelaces, or maybe go wash his face.

Faculties

Marc had scratched out his number in the phone booth with a nail file shortly after New Year's, but as things would have it, the government post-doc who had popped his cherry during office hours had passed Marc's number along to a member of his faculty, Professor Clendenin, who lived just over the suspension bridge near Cayuga Heights.

That night, Marc told his best buddies that he needed to do some reserved reading at Olin Library, but he'd be back in time to play hearts and not to start without him.

It was a twenty-minute walk past fraternity row to reach Professor Clendenin's house. Sex, she does so reduce us, Marc said to himself, the world's original coiner of sorrowful phrases, as he paused to view the drop beneath the suspension bridge. Why couldn't he admit panic before setting out, deal with it in doses, instead of forging a faux-blasé cover for it? It was early March; the rush of the snowmelt in the falls below stopped his ears, the tips of which were ready to snap off in the cold. He wasn't about to muss his hair with a hat.

His knuckles moved to the door. Professor Clendenin opened it and breathed hello onto them before he could knock. Then he whispered to Marc to keep his voice down; he'd just put his daughter to sleep. Marc nodded vigorously. For heaven's sake, he thought, let's not drag the children into this. Whereupon he tripped on an umbrella stand because his glasses were fogged up, and he'd been trying to remove his boots by feel alone in a strange hallway.

Professor Clendenin led him to a leather chair. He sat there hunched in his parka while his host went to check on baby.

Scott Clendenin was a slight man, but the library lent him great heft. Marc saw his library and fell forever in love with the way academics can live. This was the first faculty home he'd been in, Assistant Professor level, but oh, the books, the books in other languages, enough books to require alphabetization; stereo speakers with woven fronts that fit into the bookcases and were not a separate toy to consider; Javanese things, knickknacks from the field; trilobites only decorative by the by; photographs of non-family members; and art, real pieces of framed creation. Scott Clendenin was in his late twenties when they met, so he hadn't yet gathered the Scandinavian furniture and all the jazz records on the Vanguard label like his tenured superiors, but his house nevertheless bore the patina of a race of stoop-shouldered intellects who could get their groceries delivered if they choose, with wives interesting in their own right, editors or potters or bench scientists. A faculty home has a rarefied dust protecting the shafts of books, shafts of muscle to the sky, because these are the houses that books built. The books arrange the furniture to suit themselves; they decide where the woven rugs and cacti can go and lie in stacks waiting to be put back next to their neighbors. A faculty home has the scent of tatty paper slips, marking not purchases but thoughts, slips of arguments pushing out of books, new shoots from testy old orchards. A faculty home bears the soft electric buzz of Tensor lamps with round-button bulbs. A faculty home has an array of ports and liqueurs, their perfumes checked by obsidian glass stoppers crusted shut with sugars. A faculty home is full of the genuine items that launched mercantilism once upon a time: bristles that are boar; combs that are tortoise; things of bone and ivory and amber and shagreen and flax and mohair, things of gold, but also tooled in gold, inlaid with mahogany, lined in parchment, moiré fabrics doubly rare. Objects shot through with story rest on the end tables and are handled like fruit.

Marc did not know these things all at once.

Scott shared custody of three-year-old Sonya, who lived during the week with her mother in Ludlowville. The ex-wife, a high school teacher, accepted his dual sexual citizenship, awakened in Paris on a recent sabbatical semester. They remained good friends. Hearing this gave Marc the confidence to remove his parka and continue to travel the landscape, while Scott fussed with tea things. Marc didn't know the first thing about political science, save for the names of the greats that rolled so metrically off his tongue as he glossed their spines. Babeuf Bentham Hobbes Locke Mill Rousseau.

"Lemon, sugar, honey, milk?"

As he listened to Marc's life story, Scott had a tentative, left-sided smile that made Marc feel less like a callboy and more like one of his advisees. A chin cleft punctured his oval face, and his chestnut hair was silky, fine, and shoulder length. The younger one doesn't have to make the first move, this much Marc clung to, but how were their clothes going to vanish in front of this wall of knowledge? Marc stirred his tea with the silent grace of a debutante, the spoon of the bowl facing outward.

They must have sat there an hour, talking about, of all things, the history of Cornell. Finally, making an artless transition from a monologue about Mary Todd Lincoln's hand in the Morrill Land Grant Act of 1862 to Mary Todd Knell, his eighth-grade girlfriend, Marc dropped an anvil-sized hint. After weeks of going steady, the bestowal of his I.D. bracelet, and daily kissing contests on the school bus that they often won, Mary Knell (whose middle name was not Todd) dragged Marc's hand from its tense clutch around her right shoulder and placed it upon her right breast. This was during the second act of a nighttime field trip to the Ice Capades, and they were sitting a row behind their principal. After his hand had lain there twitching for several moments, Mary placed hers over his, and began moving it. From where he was, staring at the back of Mrs. Bowser's wig, he may have felt like he was groping blindly for the last gumdrops in a paper sack, but it more than satisfied Mary Knell. He'd squarely set foot on second base.

He had wanted her breasts in his hands, he confessed to Professor Clendenin, but he was the kind of boy to choke about the when of the matter.

At that, Scott got up from his station, removed Marc's glasses, and pulled him onto the couch. When the nerved carnality got so ungenteel that they tipped in a heap onto the floor, he suggested they adjourn to the bedroom.

Marc had no rhapsody to share about the faculty bedroom; he was so flushed with heat his clothes were sticking to each other as Scott undressed him. It felt a little silly for the professor to stretch on tiptoe to pull Marc's sweater over his head, but he knocked Marc out completely when, regarding him in his long johns, he murmured, "This is sexy." (No one had ever uttered this about or to Marc.) And when he slid his hand through the door of Marc's union suit and burned the small of his back with his palm, Marc had to agree. Coming undone by degrees in buttoned long underwear, it turns out, is one of winter's few rewards. They hit the hay for ninety minutes, then Marc said he had to leave.

Scott called Marc the following Wednesday at the same time.

Hearts and sex became competing priorities, with Marc setting the routine. On Fridays or Saturdays, sometimes both nights, he'd go over to Scott's after dinner at Noyes. They'd drink tea and talk for an hour, long enough for Marc to start worrying that this would be the time Scott would want *only* to talk. (Older men didn't need to do it every single time.) Scott would finally brush some hair from Marc's eye; they'd combust, hit the bedroom, and Marc would be out the door by ten-thirty. He'd whistle in the darkness, bounce-step the suspension bridge, and think of his impending hot shower all the way back to West Campus. Scrubbed and combed, he'd hitch a leg over a chair in Weker's room and play cards ferociously until three in the morning.

It's funny what a young man elects to recognize. It got so Marc might be dozing lightly in Scott's arms, then awake with a start, desperate that he'd missed the deal. He sat bolt upright the night Scott suggested that he stay overnight. The option was instantly, absolutely impossible, but Marc didn't allow himself the space to figure out why. A secret life is a secret life. It never crossed his mind to visit Scott on campus or come over even an hour earlier to have dinner with him. He assumed Scott knew better than to ask. Doubtless, Marc would have replied that he couldn't possibly miss turkey stroganoff at Noyes Dining Hall with the same six boys he had eaten his last six hundred meals with. Scott enthusiastically greeted every installment of dorm trivia as Marc checked into his settee, but Marc never once asked about the machinations of the government department. In their senior year, Weker would wind up taking Scott's Rise of Fascism seminar, but Marc never attended one of his lectures, or checked for a book Scott wrote, or even bothered to locate his office in McGraw Hall.

When they came to their last meeting, the weekend before finals and summer vacation, Scott again invited Marc to stay the night. No, he answered, but he would stay until one. Scott gave him an edition of Pascal's *Pensées* bound in Moroccan leather, since Marc was considering majoring in French and had made Scott talk more than once about his Paris sabbatical. An inscription in the flyleaf embarrassed him. His mouth went dry with shame. He said he would call in September, ruffled Scott's hair, and left. Marc might have gifted him with something in return, had he understood that this was an occasion, and that Scott correctly guessed that he wouldn't be back.

What Scott had written was that he wished he had met Marc sooner, and that eighteen and twenty-nine was not an insurmountable gap. On the walk home, Marc insisted to himself that eighteen and twenty-nine weren't even on the same planet. Scott wanted to know him better, whereas he had absorbed all the information he would ever need. For the first time, Marc felt ashamed of what he'd been up to, so much so that he knelt down on the suspension bridge and, resting his head on the grilled railing, he pushed Pascal under the suicide spokes into the falls.

The last time Marc spoke to Scott Clendenin, it was senior year. He was downtown buying a Noah's Ark set for his roommate Larry's birthday in a counterculture toy store at the Dewitt Mall. Scott's hair was shorter, and he had grown a mustache. Marc told him how handsome that made him look. Then Scott introduced Marc to Sonya, who was now six and bore his pale, oval face. Marc squatted down to talk to her, then, because his legs were shaking so badly, he kneeled outright on the floor. They chatted about all the different kinds of animals—monkeys, badgers, elephants, storks—who could fit together in the ark without getting on each other's nerves, until Marc was able to figure out that he was atoning for that windy April night freshman year when Sonya had walked into her Daddy's bedroom and asked in a sleepy voice who he was. Their eyes had locked before Marc whipped the sheet over his head, but Scott had already picked her up and, rubbing her back, told her to wave hello and goodbye to the happy ghost sitting up in the bed.

Hoo-Whee

When Kafka's *The Castle* was at last over—at this point in his life, Sam never didn't finish a book—he sped through *Nana* in a weekend. He hated Zola for destroying such voracity. He hated himself for thinking of Nana as a role model.

One afternoon in late July, with nothing to do, he trudged down from the house in the woods to the Ithaca Commons and spotted Dennis Kriesberg sunning himself against a granite plinth bearing a statue of Emma Goldman in front of the House of Shalimar. Sam couldn't remember the last time he'd seen Dennis. Even at twenty paces, he could see that Dennis's ball of red hair was still as crimped and tight as a boxwood hedge. They had been floormates their freshman year, their doors facing each other on what most of them had proudly nicknamed "The Wimpy Doubles" corridor for their collective disdain for organized athletics. Dennis went on to pledge Sigma Nu and major in mechanical engineering, so their paths never crossed. Sam figured he hadn't seen Dennis more than twice their entire junior year.

The striped athletic socks drawn to the knees clashed with the naked, hairless chest slick with suntan oil. Did he not want color on his calves and ankles? Sam cast his shadow over Dennis' face and waited. Remembering a scholarship student so physically modest he'd been ribbed for wearing a bathrobe to the showers, no matter how hot the month, Sam finally asked Dennis whether his mother approved of those obscenely skimpy swim trunks he was wearing out in public. Dennis was the only child of a widow in Queens, who'd sent weekly care packages bursting with factory seconds from the industrial bakery where she worked. Anyone with pot munchies freshman year knew where to go for appeasement.

Dennis opened his eyes and smiled to recognize his old acquaintance.

"Probably not, Sammy Boy," he said, "but Clay will want to rip them off me tonight at the radio station."

"Clay?"

"My boyfriend."

Boyfriend? They clearly had some catching up. Except for his closest female friends, Sam was still in the closet. In three years of college, he'd only had sex with two men, both pickups at the Common Ground, neither of them students, neither with any follow-through. Over sodas with Dennis at Home Dairy, he found it surprisingly easy to come out. The summertime vibe, maybe?

Sam met Clay that same evening at WVBR (*Voice of the Big Red*) in Collegetown. Clay was the station manager on weeknights, and Dennis was the deejay on the six to eleven shift. Thoughts of the double they had been sharing (twin beds, but *still*) for four semesters in the Sigma Nu house under the noses of their frat brothers were as mesmerizing to Sam as the sight of their hands crossing deftly in sync as they switched records over the platens. Their bodies touched constantly in purposeless, intimate reminders. Their voices spliced; their loud kisses reverbed in the soundproof booth. No, don't look away, they seemed to be telling Sam. This is part of your education.

Dennis signed off, but none of his ten dozen listeners were able to see Clay's tongue stuffed like a pink washrag into his ear. The trio went down to the Common Ground, at the south end of State Street, flashed their fake IDs to the bouncer, and threaded their way through a mountain pass of lesbian softballers to reach the stag line at the bar. It was 1980: half of the men, students—or student pretenders of every age—were wearing white or pink Oxford button-down shirts, sleeves folded three times to the elbow, khaki shorts, and sneakers or boat shoes without socks. Their hair was trimmed above the ears; their G & T's or scotch and sodas were set square against their solar plexuses, and ideally, their grosgrain belts matched their watch straps.

The townie half of the population was wearing jewel-toned wife-beaters, or filmy sports shirts tucked into Daisy Duke cutoff shorts, their flesh adorned by random parures of rings, bracelets, chain necklaces, and stud earrings. Their hair was longer—shag cuts, unironic mullets, even a few daring, if dated, permanent waves; and they pooched their lips to drain colorful cocktails through straws.

A spilled drink in a public house needn't be a catastrophe. Should you dash your scotch onto someone else's shirt or trousers, simply offer a professional cleaning. Or let it dry, then assess the damage. Gilbert de la Hunta, whose left thigh Sam reflexively blotted with paper napkins, would claim the spill was a great way for Sam to make a pass. It was too noisy inside to converse, so Gilbert pointed Sam to the rear exit. Sam handed his empty glass and the wad of wet napkins to a grinning Dennis Kriesberg.

Sam had never been out back of the Common Ground, which was no more than a rectangular asphalt pen furnished with three wooden cable spools. The men moving on each other like inchworms against the chain link fence upped Sam's mortification. He apologized over and over, looking everywhere—bricks, weeds, shoes—except at the aggrieved party and his wet thigh. When he was finally calm enough to focus on Gilbert's face, he inventoried an olive complexion, thin lips, hazel eyes, a widow's peak over a strong brow, a protagonist's jaw, and a nose cut the way precious stones are. With a family name like de La Hunta, he could be the dashing scion of an old Castilian family. He was very attractive.

Sam didn't know what came over him, certainly not the few pre-spill swallows of his drink, but when Patsy Cline's "Walking After Midnight," a romantic change-up from the diet of disco and New Wave tunes for the dancing fools inside, drifted through the loudspeakers, Sam let himself be kissed. It had been a very long time. The careful softness of Gil's mouth, and his *quiet* lips (as he would later confess to Dennis) were a revelation.

With their free hands, they waved goodbye to Dennis and Clay, then necked out of doors on a bench under a river birch at Stewart Park. The waves lapped at the shore of Lake Cayuga, the locusts kept up a steady susurrus, Gil seemed manly and uncomplicated, pressuring nothing beyond kissing and nuzzling, and Sam felt happy.

To experience more of the same, he agreed to go camping with Gil at Buttermilk Falls that weekend.

"Camping, huh?" said Billy, Sam's housemate, looking at him with something of his old rudeness when Sam asked to borrow his sleeping bag.

"I've gone camping before," Sam answered.

"Who with?"

"My mother and a man she was dating at the time."

"No dork, who are you going to Buttermilk Falls with?"

"Dennis Kriesberg and some friends of his," Sam lied.

"*Kriesberg*?" Billy started laughing. He too had been part of the Wimpy Doubles corridor freshman year and remembered Kriesberg as a pathetic mama's boy. "Is he working on a Girl Scout Badge?"

"Sure you don't want to go?"

Sam was pleased to make Billy laugh. He'd been having a rotten summer too.

Gilbert took care of the tent and the provisions. Sam, as instructed, packed some warm things. For most of the drive to Buttermilk Falls, he rested his head in Gil's lap. Under someone else's steering wheel seemed a fair indication of his emotional placement. Maybe it was the aftertaste of Zola, or Dennis and Clay's rutty tandem display, but a nearly lunatic need for touch had surfaced in him.

Gil pitched the tent in a designated clearing. Their sleeping bags easily zipped together. They christened this piece of luck with more ravenous necking, then set off on a hike.

The trees, the trail, and the actual falls largely escaped Sam's attention, but every forty paces on the forest floor, he'd tug, or Gil would, at the basket of hands they'd made, a reminder to kiss and to hold each other close, a renewal amidst the chirps and rustles and twig snaps of their, of their what? Of their boldness, of their liberation, of their oneness with the wood thrushes and the chipmunks? All Sam knew was he was living for the next embrace. At one stop, he said to Gil, "Nature's the best setting for sex. You can put it on my tombstone."

It was a joke, but Gil's expression was so odd that Sam pulled his face to his in order to blot out the thought he had begun to decipher in his eyes.

There was a sudden crack of branches. They came unclasped, but not before they heard a sickening whoop: "Hoo-whee, would you look at that? Two guys kissing!" a hog call of incredulity that seemed to echo for minutes in the pines.

Moving towards them was a teenage boy carrying a fishing rod and a dumpy female companion with a tackle box. Their paths would have to cross. Sam couldn't look at them as they stepped off the trail and let them pass.

Sam heard their laughter for yards, can hear it to this day—and he can summon them too, a pair of Tompkins County crackers with an ignorant opinion. Their disgust shocked him more than their discovery. The boy hadn't *thought* to say that; his truth had flown out clean. His jeer was a punch to the gut. Sam needed to sit against a tree, his hand clamped to Gil's calf, to settle his stomach.

Now that they were taboo in those parts, instead of slinking back into town, their ardor redoubled in the camp clearing. To offset his shame, Sam ostentatiously chewed every mouthful of corn, tore at his burgers, and dared the other campers to wonder at what noises they might be making in the night. Naturally, no one paid them the slightest bit of attention.

Later, in the sleeping bag, after a first bout of joyful, actual, fluid-exchanging sex, Gil told Sam his story: taken at eleven on a regular schedule by older boys at his fancy boarding school. Unwanted attentions from his piano teacher. After a year of being fondled on the bench, he told another teacher about *her*. He, not she, was removed from the school. His parents never believed him. His shrink believed him, maybe.

Sam now knew more about Gilbert de la Hunta than he did about Billy or Conrad or any Wimpy Doubler, or his brother Wyatt, who had lived on the other side of Sam's bedroom wall for fourteen years. He turned on the flashlight to assess the damage. Too inexperienced that night to know that emotional divestiture can be an act of aggression, Sam fell into Gil's arms.

Sam woke to the smell of coffee through the open tent flaps. Gil was as composed as ever. No one had to tell Sam he'd been keeping watch over him since sunup.

"I love you, Sam," he said.

Sam was horrified. "Don't say that. You don't know me."

"I love you," Gil repeated.

"NO!" shouted Sam. Someone shifted in the next tent, so he lowered his voice. "I don't know you. I like you a lot."

"You don't have to love me back."

Sam recoiled at the thought.

"I don't love you, Gil. And—"

Then came the second dawn of the day.

"What, Sam? And what?"

Sam wanted to run from the tent, weighted, burdened with Gil's need, but did not. "I could never love you now" was what he wanted to say, but he held his tongue.

Gil began to cry. Sam was the nicest man he'd met in Ithaca. He couldn't help falling in love with him when he'd made him so happy. "I'm barely more than a boy!" Sam wanted to scream, *"Where did you get your information?"* But, knowing just where, he held Gil for a long, last time, and then they struck the tent.

Cufflinks

The night after the cookout, Boyd and Kurt were alone in the house, sweltering in shotgun-mad-dog-August-heat-rash heat. Their house-mates had gone bowling. As a going-away present, Kurt gave Boyd a pair of silver cufflinks, their oval faces embossed with bright blue, enameled fleurs-de-lis.

"I don't have shirts with French cuffs," said Boyd.

"It doesn't matter," Kurt said. "It was just an impulse."

Kurt decided not to reveal the second, identical pair, which he'd bought with the notion that they'd wear them together through the years to weddings, christenings, and funerals. They were rolled in a pair of socks in his carry-on, tucked under a stairwell by the front door with his other two bags.

"I didn't get you anything," said Boyd.

"I don't care. You've given me plenty."

Boyd rolled his eyes.

"You're drunk," Kurt said to shut down the matter of the blown gift exchange.

"No more than you."

"You've sucked down five to my two," Kurt answered. That was their beer ratio that sophomore year, and the hell with you, he thought, for making him sound like some B-movie moll.

Boyd shook the cufflinks in his hands like a pair of dice, then set them quietly in his ashtray. "Don't go to Germany."

Kurt had been yearning for this very directive their entire, miraculous, only-come-up-for-air week between the sheets. He wasn't certain Boyd would say this, but he'd prepared a response.

"I have to go. It's paid for."

Boyd had thought about it too. "So, get your money back."

Kurt flipped a pillow, still damp from their sweating necks. "Boyd," he said, "when you run out of underwear, and you don't feel like doing your laundry, you buy new in packages of three, don't you? Don't you?"

His vehemence was a surprise to both of them.

"What is *that* supposed to mean?"

"Your parents keep you in underwear. They keep you in everything."

"What are we talking about my parents for?"

"You don't know the value of a dollar."

"You're going to Frankfurt on your father's money."

"His life insurance."

There was no comeback for that, so Boyd left the room, picking his way through the empties and the twisted bedclothes on the floor. Kurt pulled on his polo and shorts, listening to the moths beat against the screen under the deck lamp, to the closing of the refrigerator door, to the flip of a cap in the sink.

Boyd returned with beer number six. "What are you getting dressed for?"

Kurt kept still while Boyd unbuttoned his shirt again. Funny way to have an argument. Kurt asked him whether he was going to miss him while he was in Europe.

Boyd dragged Kurt's belt through its loops. "I'm planning to be miserable without you. You're my best friend. I love you. I even *like* you, which is saying a lot, considering what an asshole you are ninety percent of the time."

Boyd had cleared a bar without knowing it, so Kurt raised it again. "I want you to love me sober too."

"Help me out here," Boyd said, fumbling with the fly. "I *am* drunk."

Kurt popped the placket on his shorts. "You better be careful, or you'll be a serious alcoholic."

"Are there unserious alcoholics?"

Kurt pushed Boyd's hands away. "You'll make a lousy drunk. I know all about it."

That last flew out of his mouth, and it made him feel rotten. In high school, after dinner, Kurt's father would tour their subdivision with an open bottle of Cutty Sark. If he wasn't back by the time Kurt had finished his trig proofs, it was his job to find out which neighbor's living room floor he'd conked out on and bring him home. Kurt would flick his father's ear with his index finger until he woke up. His mother said when they cut him open, his liver was the size of a Smithfield ham.

Kurt looked at Boyd, bent on the mattress now like a twisted-open paper clip. Drunk or sober, he was all Kurt wanted or had or gone after, and now they were going to be apart for ten months. He folded Boyd against his chest, then laced their fingers together on the neck of the beer bottle. In the heat, the glass had already reached room temperature.

"I'm afraid of you," Boyd whispered.

This was news to sit up for, but Kurt stayed put.

"When you fell asleep on my floor in April, and I realized that I loved you, I was terrified of what would happen when you woke up."

"I'm sorry I made you fall for me," said Kurt.

Boyd rolled out of his grasp. "You didn't *make* me love you, Kurt. I mean sure, I fell in love with a man, but give me some credit here." His laugh became a belch. "You're the one who's gay."

"No, I'm not," said Kurt. "I'm bisexual."

Boyd started laughing. "That's what *I* used to say, remember?"

Kurt did remember. That had cracked open a door for them at the end of freshman year.

"And then you came at me, with all your might." Boyd swigged, belched again. "All your mighty might might."

They were facing each other on the bed, kneeling, naked, at odds, the mattress radiating heat like a portal to Hades. It had taken Kurt sixteen months to get them to this position, but Boyd was looking at him like he was some idiot child. With clumsy fingers, he brushed Kurt's arm and said, "Came at me hammer and tongs."

With no thought at all, Kurt raised a fist and clubbed him in the jaw. Then, because he loved his face, he clubbed it again. Then, a slap, which made a cleaner sound. Boyd looked surprised more than anything. His hands, which he'd put up in front of his face for defense, suddenly, as if a toy spring had been pushed, flopped at the wrists.

Rather than handcuff him, as his pose suggested, Kurt ran into the kitchen. He opened the fridge and crouched in its cold air, rattling his teeth on the lip of the pitcher of iced tea he drained. He couldn't claim to have hurt him—his hand probably smarted more than Boyd's jaw— but enjoying the violence had scared the piss out of him.

Eyes fixed on a bowl of salt potatoes from the cookout, Kurt rewrote fisticuffs into folklore. He must really love the rummy if he could also want to break his jaw. This was men loving men like men must love men, proof more positive than matching cufflinks. He closed the refrigerator and slumped against it, waiting for Boyd to come fetch him. After five minutes, inflated with apologies, horny with reconciliation, Kurt went back to the bedroom.

Boyd had passed out on his stomach.

Kurt's anger really lit up when he realized Boyd wouldn't remember and respect the violence of their fight. He wasn't about to beat a drunk into consciousness, so, with a passion equal to his slaps, he began to jerk off onto Boyd's back. Strokes for being drunk, for being a drunk, for being rich, for having both parents intact, for forgetting, for being honest, for taking Kurt up, for doing as he liked, for taking charge of himself, for getting out of hand, and—for—not—being—him.

Kurt left him to dry and fell asleep.

He woke up flooded with remorse. Kurt reached out his hands, gimme, but the air was empty.

It was already light outside. Boyd was smoking at his desk chair, dressed and shod, watching Kurt with an expression that increased his panic and killed all comment.

"Did you hit me?"

His face bore no marks of it, but he had remembered.

"I think you hit me, Kurt."

Kurt wouldn't have the man anywhere near him for a year, couldn't track his movements, couldn't fill his days with him. You cannot leave this room, he thought; you have got to come back to this bed.

Interpreting Kurt's silence, but one beat ahead, Boyd ground out his cigarette, picked up his keys and left. The slam of the front door covered Kurt's wail.

His memory of recent events put it into Kurt's head that Boyd was leaving *him* forever, and that his was an exit more final than airplanes. Not until he heard the car start and pull out of the turnaround was he able to mobilize. He ran out of the house at five in the morning after a red Opel rustling through a stand of overgrown sumacs.

And as he ran naked down a rural route in upstate New York, he waved his arms and screamed, not caring who saw or heard him, he could cash his ticket, sweet Jesus, just stop the car, Boyd, so they could banish fear and live on love. He was running so fast he couldn't sense anything but motion; he ran out the rest of the violence he thought he'd reasoned away the night before by the refrigerator; he was so crazed he put on an extra burst of speed to outrun the coronary that had stopped his father and that he knew was waiting for him too, somewhere up the blacktop. He didn't know how long or how far he ran in his bare feet after Boyd, but he was so jacked up that he didn't notice that the car had stopped until he had nearly overtaken it.

Boyd opened the passenger door.

"Don't leave me like that," gasped Kurt, pulling it shut and slumping against the window. He jerked upright at the press of the cold glass on his shoulder. "Don't leave me," he said with all the air he had left for speech.

"I was going for cigarettes."

Before the car could move again, they knew they would have to process the spectacle of Kurt's need. Boyd had sunk him this low; he could own that part of him, but not everything, still not everything. Kurt rolled down the window for a view, gulped air, waiting reconnaissance. The birds were making a racket, but the trees and the wind kept their counsel.

Boyd reached over to touch Kurt's neck. Kurt did not trust himself to look at Boyd, and so looked down instead.

He looked down and saw that he wasn't naked. Somehow, in Boyd's room, in the haste and terror he'd felt as his car spun the rocks behind it to hit the road, Kurt managed to locate his briefs and throw them on.

One gesture toward modesty, at the last of the last of the last, let him know that there would still be further to fall.

Part Two
Parting Shots

"Run for the roundhouse Nellie, and you might corner him there."

Coil

I've been a theater professor at Haverford College outside Philadelphia for a long time. As the years pile up, and I perceive with increasing clarity the anvils suspended above each one of their sleek, unmarked heads, I feel the urge to offer my students personal advice. This generally happens at the end of a "life versus art" logjam that a five-hour dramatic literature seminar can provoke. While they re-calibrate, back to the plot and the characters—who, I remind them, are not people, but *vessels of action*—I float notions: At least once in their lives, they must recklessly cross the country, or better still, an ocean, for love. The woman of quality will have had one boyfriend who turned out to be gay. Never marry a therapist. The fit on a dance belt should be snug, not tight. Never sleep with someone just because you dreamed about it. High school is never over. Children are not an abstraction.

Whether my off-syllabus convictions are absorbed is beside the point. I am a middle-aged, tenured smorgasbord of white cis-male privilege, so no one is looking at me. My undergraduates have time only (and justly) for their own agons, but you might have a moment to hear how, on the weekend of my 30th birthday, I recklessly flew from Rhode Island to Seattle for love.

"I'm in a fucking hotel room, Kitty!" I wailed into the phone.

"What? Roger? A what?"

Forgetting the time difference, I had woken Kitty up when I thought she'd be watching the World Series. She'd gotten her MFA in acting in Minneapolis and was a rabid Twins fan.

"He put me in a hotel room."

"Who did? Conrad?"

Her "Conrad?" sounded like "carbad." It wasn't the connection or the hour. A deviated septum repair the week before had occluded her voice. The breathing straws had only just come out of her nose. Residual bruising around the eyes made her look like a sadistic boyfriend's punching bag.

"Yes, Conrad! He picked me up at the airport, drove me to dinner with his designers, I watched his preview, gave him notes, and he dropped me off at a fucking Marriott."

Room 307, to be exact, whose color scheme was beef tongue and apricot jam and had a view of the dumpsters.

"Did you make out in the car?"

"Not one kiss," I said. "Or even a hand-hold. Nothing."

"Oh honey, I'm sorry." I heard Kitty shifting around. A bleat I heard meant she'd pushed her orange tabby, Oscar, whom she claimed to hate, off her bed.

"There's still tomorrow, right?"

"He's going to pick me up at nine to have breakfast at Pike's Market."

"You have all day to be his tampon then."

"But I wanted it to be tonight."

"I know, Roger. I know."

I wanted to turn thirty screwing my brains out with a hot, brand-new lover. I yanked open the nightstand drawer and slid the promotional brochures into it. I wasn't a tourist. I was on my first-ever romantic assignation. Just riffling the pages of my Fed-Exed round-trip ticket had given me hard-ons.

"How was the show?" she asked.

"What?"

"How was *Much Ado*?"

I stifled the urge to ask Kitty whose side she was on. Conrad Bosek was directing *Much Ado About Nothing* at Seattle Repertory Theatre. It wasn't a play I knew well. Conrad had laughed over the phone when I'd said I would be coming before his production as would a child. That would actually help me a lot, Roger, he'd replied, softening his voice to the conspiratorial timbre that made me drench my boxer shorts every time he called, which had been pretty much four nights out of seven, ten o'clock my time, nine o'clock his, for the last five months.

"Terrific," I admitted. "He's a really good director, what can I say?" I paused to search for a negative. "Dogberry comes on way too late. I'd cut him." No fan of Shakespeare's roisterers, I had decided while watching the preview that Dogberry was a close second to Autolycus in *The Winter's Tale* in the Lame Clown Sweepstakes.

"You can't cut Dogberry," said Kitty. "He arrests Borrachio and brings him to Don Pedro."

"If you say so."

"How were Beatrice and Benedick?"

"Hilarious," I said in a tone so sour it made her laugh.

Two clues—the tampon and the paper ticket—point us to the early 1990's. In a leaked phone conversation that helped end his first marriage, King Charles III of England had fantasized to Camilla Parker Bowles, today Her Royal Highness Queen Consort, "I'll just lie inside your trousers or something," and even better, that he'd like to be her Tampax. Everything was grist for Kitty and me, and our minds rarely strayed from the gutter. À propos of nothing, I'd suddenly announce at work, "Ich bin Connies Tampon."

"Ach ja, du bist Connies Tampon," she'd fire back.

Our use of German referred to Charles' Saxe-Coburg-Gotha family line. The change from Conrad to Connie is more complicated; it's both an homage to songstress Connie Francis, sexually assaulted in a Long Island motor lodge in 1974, and to "coney," Elizabethan slang for rabbit—and vagina.

As for the plane ticket, before the Internet, there were places called travel agencies staffed by people called travel agents who would search for available flights on absurd little desk monitors that blinked green letters and numbers. Purchases were printed in red-inked carbon triplicate. That I was flying to a strange city on someone else's dime to *be with him* was romantic enough. That the ticket arrived *overnight* in a FedEx envelope addressed to Mr. Roger Hauf the day before takeoff was a double dose of Spanish Fly. Only important people with vital, urgent business received FedExes.

That was me, with a vital urge that spanned three time zones. Conrad Bosek was ten years older than I was, a burly Polish American from a working-class family in Maryland, who was a big deal in the American non-profit theater. So butch and so circumspect, no one knew whether he was actually gay or actually straight or possibly both. I, on the other hand, don't pass and never did. Middle school sissies and fruits follow their stars to become college faggots and lifetime fairies. (No pushback about stereotypes, please. I *own* this one, from a Minton Rose service for ten to the "Ella Fitzgerald Sings the Rodgers & Hart Songbook" I bought at the age of twenty.)

When I met Conrad Bosek, I had finished my coursework for a doctorate at Brown, passed my orals, and had had my topic—Seneca's Influence on the Jacobeans—approved. Somewhat stagestruck, and refractory at the time to sustained research, I had taken a pause in the PhD process. A sympathetic advisor cued me to a six-month literary internship at Trinity Rep, and I got the gig. I had proved so useful to Conrad's production of *Julius Caesar* that Trinity re-hired me in the fall, now with a stipend that supplemented what I earned leading undergrad sections of Brit Lit: *Beowulf* to Boswell.

Extending my leave to spend another half-year in show business worried my doctoral committee and my parents, both academics. I was covertly hoping for a permanent position at Trinity Rep. Caitlin "Kitty" Brooks was my office confidante. She was a marketing associate, a pay grade above mine; our windowless cubicles with doors faced each other across a hall. Her housebound mother was chaining her to Providence until she croaked or could be put into a facility. Then Kitty was going to do "the New York actor thing." "How's your mother?" I'd ask most mornings, and Kitty would answer, "Extant," a routine akin to our 'Conrad's tampon' exchange.

I was assigned to *Julius Caesar* because of my Renaissance lit background. My rehearsal duties included consulting Schmidt's *Shakespeare Lexicon,* and Furness' *New Variorum* of *Julius Caesar* to offer to the actors an array of possible meanings and intentions for obscure words and phrases. I also prepared a moderately exhaustive "dramaturgy packet" of information about Roman civilization and the Caesars. My surprise obligation was to have dinner with Conrad Bosek every night after rehearsal. His home base was Chicago, so the first week I assumed that he was lonely and needed an audience. Then, I thought he was taking pity on a cash-strapped grad student and novice dramaturg. He always picked up the check, which I found gallant until Kitty revealed he had a *per diem*.

But then I had my upper left third molar removed. To this day, I can hear and feel the echo of the crack inside my skull when the dentist separated the tooth from my jaw with a swift twist of what had looked like a dandelion weeder. I insisted on keeping the tooth. Kitty drove me home. Singing along to R.E.M., I kept turning its blocky, buttermilk strangeness in my fingers and sniffing the secret stench emanating from a lentil-sized hole in the crown. Had that really come out of me? I placed the wisdom tooth into a brass twist tobacco box embossed with CYMRU, which means Wales, alongside two other treasures: a sixties scarab pin I had lifted from my mother's jewelry box, and a two-inch stone fragment taken illegally from the Roman Forum by my best friend, David Towle.

Kitty was heating instant cream of leek soup, balm for my throbbing jaw, in my kitchen when the phone rang. It was Conrad, calling from rehearsal.

"How's my patient doing?" he asked. Not *the* patient. *My* patient.

"I'm pretty zonked on painkillers," I said. "No complications, knock wood. How's rehearsal going?"

"It's not the same without you." Did he really say that?

"Do you need anything, Roger? I can swing by after we finish here."

"No, I'm cool. I appreciate the offer though." He hadn't a clue as to where I lived.

"Don't come tomorrow if you don't feel up to it."

"I'll be there."

"Okay then."

As soon as he'd said *my* patient, what I needed was sexual release. I covered my crotch with a *Newsweek* as Kitty brought in the bowls of Knorr. We parsed and replayed that eight-line conversation umpteen times, switching parts and making endless salacious variations for "my" "complications" "wood" "need" "Roger" "swing" "come" "up to it" and even "okay." Kitty's ruling—I must wait for Conrad to make the first move—was a relief. The secretary doesn't hit on the boss. Moreover, I never made first moves.

That doesn't mean the secretary doesn't flirt with the boss. I upped my dinner game during Conrad's final two weeks in Providence. This isn't easy to explain. I had never questioned my basic intelligence, or my capacity for intellection, but Conrad Bosek made me feel smart in a way no other person ever had. The intensity of his attention slayed me. He paid no compliments, never referred to matters of the heart or asked personal questions, but the quality of his banter was captivating; he drew me into a world of cultural and literary reference, with anecdotes about stage misfires and actor egos, interspersed with side comments that demonstrated an offhand mastery of history, philosophy, political theory, world religions, and the Western poetic canon. Imagine a butch Noël Coward with *depth*. Where he led, I followed, or did my best to keep up. Conrad needed an audience, but he made of me a near-equal. Under his spotlight, fueled by Sidecars and wine and three courses every night, I felt dazzling as I never had before, and never would again. Conrad wasn't handsome, but the more attention he paid, the sexier I found him. If I couldn't *be* him, I would sleep with him and, his thick arms tucked around my chest, I would absorb his knowledge in the night. I would grow to become his attribute.

As the *Julius Caesar* opening approached, our conversations grew more technical; I gave him notes about pace and articulation, notes that he copied out in a heavy, flowing script from a fountain pen; when tech period started, the designers joined us at dinner, and I'd be simultaneously torn between feeling special—one of the team, his team—and feeling jealous when his spotlight found someone else. I assumed the moment would arrive, in the theater or backstage or in the prop shop, when he would press me to a wall and kiss me until I passed out, but no matter how much I loitered with intent, it never happened. Even with the clock running out, the secretary does not hit on the boss.

For opening night, Conrad wrote me a note saying he hoped we'd collaborate again, ideally on a comedy, and signed it, "All best." At the post-show party, I couldn't compete with the trustees, academics, and actors who mobbed him. With an early flight to catch, he slipped out, probably while I was re-loading at the buffet. (I'm not an actor, but I eat like one.)

✳

He'd left on a Friday. The first phone call was Tuesday; how was the show doing, and had there been any interesting patron feedback at the post-show discussions I was hosting? By the 1990's, the Post-Modern production wave had struck the non-profit Shakespeare beach: Weimar *Measure for Measures*, *Twelfth Night* goes Hawaiian, Olmec *Richard IIIs*, etc. Conrad's visual equivalent for Imperial Rome was Kennedy's Camelot. The men wore suits with narrow ties; a pink pillbox hat accessorized Portia's Chanel suit. The Roman Senate was the DC Senate floor. If I could remember some of the more subtle parallels we worked out for this structurally untidy tragedy, I could make the Bosek *Caesar* seem less of a novelty and more of the well-spoken, coherent, gripping, and popular revelation it was to Trinity audiences and Rhode Island critics alike.

Conrad's calls averaged ninety minutes. If he skipped a night, he'd provide a reason the next night. Trained all through school by Jesuits, he spoke in long, periodic sentences, timed his pauses should I require a footnote. I kept a running list by the phone of the books and writers he mentioned. I fantasized that our lopsided Socratic dialogues cloaked his arousal too.

Living alone for the first time, I was renting a three-room, first-floor apartment in a ratty clapboard triple-decker. The carved fireplace surround matched the dentil molding. When unfolded for sleep, my queen-sized futon—off the ground (at last) in an unpainted pine frame Kitty and I had bought at Pier One—ended two feet from my front door, which opened onto the central hallway. That winter I heard every pair of snow boots enter and exit the building. Some nights Conrad's voice felt so warm and so close, I imagined I had only to spring the lock and wait for him to fall and crush me in bed, word made flesh, with his massive body of knowledge.

Spring became summer; the azaleas and the peonies came and went; the boots turned to flip-flops. Still he talked and, over the staccato hum of my standing fan, still I listened, without a single intimate exchange. The laughs I managed to generate in him were my triumphs; my gratification lay in believing that mine was the last voice Conrad needed to hear before he went to bed. AIDS was raging, and with only one drug, AZT, approved for treatment, I reasoned it might be worth living inside the notion that high-minded talk was a mature advance over physical connection. When the cure was found, our sexual congress would be all the better for having been delayed. And how infinitely hotter to combust in a fire laid with the tinder and logs of Shakespeare, Kant, St. Ignatius of Loyola, and Elizabeth Bishop.

Mornings at work, Kitty and I would re-twist the Bosek Rubik's Cube. She was sleeping with Trinity's Technical Director, a guy so smitten to have found a woman who would have sex every night *and* put her mouth on it without argument or negotiation, he wanted her to move in after two weeks. (That, she'd sighed, was the downside of head on demand.) Kitty was losing patience with my situation. Her theories that I was Conrad's psych experiment, that he had a micro-penis, total body eczema, a live-in girlfriend, a secret ecclesiastical lover—were amusing to spin, but I would simply tell her that she didn't know the man the way I did.

Kitty's triple-decker shared an alley with a gay club called Buddies. After last call, she could hear men having summertime sex below her bedroom window, a sound she likened to someone stirring a bowl of potato salad. Her new ruling: Conrad was no longer my boss; I was either to emit a clear romantic or erotic signal, my choice, in a phone call, or visit Buddies with her and make potato salad with a stranger.

My passivity had begun to bore Kitty, and I couldn't have that. I split her difference: one Saturday night I lied to Conrad, saying that I had gone out to Buddies post-phone call the night before and had had several Sidecars in his honor. The next night, during a pause, Conrad abruptly murmured, in his husky register, "You know what's happening, don't you?"

I paused. "Yes, I do." I paused again. "I want it to happen."

"Ahh," he exhaled.

That was it. Rather than explore the topic, I allowed him to drop it, secure—not to mention over the moon—with the knowledge that it was going to happen. Decades later, I finally saw *Brief Encounter,* Noël Coward's masterpiece of British sublimation, only eclipsed after forty-seven years by *The Remains of the Day.* Trevor Howard's grave, sudden, "You know what's happened, don't you?" and Celia Johnson's reply, "Yes. Yes, I do," struck me as utter camp until I realized that Conrad and I had shared almost the exact exchange, just not in a train depot.

Conrad began rehearsing *Much Ado About Nothing* in Seattle in August; the extra time zones meant fewer electric conversations. When he floated the notion of flying me out to see him on preview weekend in early October, I was so excited that I first had to pretend I didn't understand the offer, which I knew fell outside any *per diem.* Then I had to pretend that he was joking. Then, as casually as an avalanche, I said I would consult my calendar. How had the man known it was my birthday weekend?

One hitch: at the same time as Conrad was previewing *Much Ado,* my boss's boss, the Trinity Rep Artistic Director, was previewing her production of Clifford Odets' *Golden Boy.* I was supposed to take a batch of notes at the Saturday preview and give them to my actual boss, the Resident Dramaturg, who would then pass the ones he agreed with on to her.

Kitty took charge of covering my butt. Merely calling in sick didn't appeal to her sense of drama. Wired for make-believe, she would relay my escalating pulmonary distress at work on Friday, then at Saturday's *Golden Boy* preview. My job was to lay up in Conrad's bed all weekend, rising only for servings of ambrosia and royal jelly. Leaving work on Thursday, I told my boss that I was wheezy and feared running a temperature.

After my distress call to Kitty, I slept fitfully. On day two in Seattle, my 30th birthday, the weather was chilly and cloudless. Conrad and I had a standing cappuccino at a stall in Pike's Market, then breakfast at a restaurant overlooking Pioneer Square. Parking ate up a lot of time.

Conversation did not flow. We had only been in enclosed spaces before; it was difficult to get any kind of groove going outdoors. As if on an awkward first date, I looked at the sidewalk, and he checked out storefronts. For a man that bulky, he had delicate ankles and small feet, always shod in tasseled loafers. We drifted through a couple of used bookstores. When I realized we were not going to go back to artist housing to wreck his sheets, I visited a more comforting location—my past. I counted back to my twentieth birthday, when I was a junior in college. The boy I was in love with and I were having the sort of misunderstanding you have when you are about ten days off from that first, fevered fuck. His present was a bottle of Amaretto. As I removed it from its box, he said, "See, it has a square top, Roger, that you can shove up your ass." Then I rewound back to my tenth birthday. Fifth grade. A photo exists of me in a bowl cut that accentuates my moon face. Gay as a picnic basket, I am wearing groovy striped trousers and a ribbed, mustard polo shirt that laced instead of buttoned up the throat. With outstretched Jesus hands, I am blessing my father's gift, a freestanding chessboard made of plastic wood, its pieces molded in a medieval treatment.

Conrad bought me a used copy of *The Magic Lantern,* Ingmar Bergman's autobiography, a big influence on his work, he said. Maybe I was Eliza Doolittle. Maybe he was straight. Erudition was suddenly less sexy. I napped at the Marriott until he picked me up for a second dinner with his design team. I put the costume and the lighting designer between us at the table. If I hadn't been so invested in my sulk, I might have plied them with Conrad questions and learned something useful.

Dogberry proved no less tiresome on a second go with *Much Ado.* Again, I sat in on the notes session. (Conrad was my ride home, after all.) Listening to the thoughts that Seattle Rep dramaturg, Mark Dakota, had for Conrad was a master class for me in practical criticism. I told Mark as much as the meeting broke. Throwing me a bone, he thanked me for my insight about the word "coil." At some point, Ursula says to Beatrice, "Madam, you must come to your uncle. Yonder's/ old coil at home." The reference confused me. Both nights I had thought that "old coil" was a character named Coil who the audience never got to meet.

Processing my observation—another county heard from—Conrad and Mark had shared a quick look of what I read as condescension.

Mark explained that 'coil' meant 'turmoil' or 'confusion."

I thought for a moment. "You could say 'mess' then, instead of 'coil." I replied. "Yonder's a mess at home."

"Well observed and duly noted," said Conrad, one of his consistent laugh lines.

I called Kitty from Room 307 that second night too. If this happened today, I could just send her a text string of emojis signifying fury, loss, shame, and humiliation.

✳

My flight left at 6:20 a.m. At the Marriott desk, the attendant said, "You're good to go, Mr. Hauf." I didn't need to sign anything. Just like a rent boy. Had the weekend gone as anticipated, I would have dined out on the analogy.

There was a rime of frost on the median grass, and on the car windows in the parking lot. Conrad was blowing into his hands when I tossed my bag into the back seat.

Sea-Tac Airport is a straight shot south of the city. Conrad was cheerful, hearty, making up for my silence with more *Much Ado*. He had thought it over and decided to replace "old coil" with "a mess." (I had made my mark after all.) Maybe he wanted me to thank him, or say "on with the show," or "just doing my bit." What if I'd said I jerked off every time we hung up the phone? What if I'd told him that I had turned thirty the day before?

We cleared the entrance. I was watching people wrestle luggage pieces out of car hatches in an intense, clothes-flapping wind when Conrad's voice took on its bewitching, late-night tone:

"I know this isn't how we wanted it to be."

[and...] "I should have planned better."

[and...] "I get so wrapped up in my work I can't focus on anything else."

These three statements had enough room in between them to permit my mind to flood with forgiveness. "I understand," I replied.

"Do you, Rog?"

I nodded, opened the door, and got out, bearing a huge, helpless smile at his first use of my diminutive—a brilliant directorial touch. My hair blew straight up in the wind like a referee signaling "Touchdown!"

"Talk soon?" he said.

I pulled my bag from the back seat, then made a little wave as his rental pulled away.

What timing. From the "Welcome to Sea-Tac Airport" sign, to my drop-off at the United Terminal, Conrad had had only the length of a football field in which to reel me back in. An hour later, sailing through a magnificent, snow-crested vista of the Rocky Mountains, worthy of *National Geographic* and "The Hallelujah Chorus," Ich war Connies Tampon all over again.

Kitty picked me up in Providence, and we replayed the highlights reel at a Thai birthday dinner. (Odd to recall that Thai was once the newest cuisine on the block.)

While I was on romantic assignment, my apartment had been broken into. A robbery *does* feel like a violation. The thief had cut the screen on my open bathroom window, climbed through, and made a coil of my belongings. Drawers and cabinets, closets and bookcases, the refrigerator, potted plants, everything I owned had been pitched to the floor. I recall being surprised at how little I had accumulated at thirty, but trust me when I say there was nothing valuable besides my great-grandmother's silver ewer, now gone, as were the CD player and speakers (leaving me the obsolescing turntable) and a brass tobacco box that contained a scarab pin, a fragment of the Roman Forum, and one dead wisdom tooth. I threw bath towels on the spilled milk, juice, and coffee grounds in the kitchen, then called in a police report, an effort one makes, however futilely, to tie the bow on these sorts of hefty dramatic reversals.

Monday after lunch, my boss, just off a phone call with Seattle Rep peer Mark Dakota, called me in to ask what I was doing taking notes at *Much Ado About Nothing* previews instead of taking notes at *Golden Boy*? My facetious answer would have been that I had been doing field research, but he fired me before I could say anything.

I went to my office and packed up my effects. I had gotten canned without getting laid, a miscarriage of justice that led me to kick two feet of new play submissions stacked beside my desk. They crashed against the wastepaper basket and nearly tipped it over. Her door was closed, but I could hear Kitty nimbly hectoring someone over the phone. She would rise over the years to become Trinity Rep's first female managing director. If extant today, her ailing mother would be in her late eighties. We still exchange holiday greetings.

Cotton Mather and his kind preached that the theater and its practitioners were ubiquitous instruments of Satan. This sexless sack is the how and the when and the why I decided to stay clear of show business and complete that doctorate on "Seneca and the Jacobeans." My dissertation became my first book, which helped with tenure, and there you have it, here we are.

In summing up my reckless, country-crossing love, which kept up (I kid you not) for an additional *year*, through productions of both *Mary Stuart* and *Glengarry Glen Ross,* one in Providence, the other in Atlanta—same song, different verse, dozens of dinners, not one kiss— I've managed to convince myself that Conrad Bosek's refusal to, quoting a tune of the era, "get physical," wasn't because of me. I think he was terrified of what his body wanted, and what might happen to him should he permit it to have what it wanted. Time and experience have also allowed me to understand that had I managed to coax him out of his clothes, even if only down to an undershirt, he would have done his best to obliterate me. Better in the end that our wave never crested, better that what was happening never happened.

I could recite for you Whitman's "I Saw in Louisiana a Live-Oak Growing," a copy of which was my final communication to the man, but I fear you've run out of patience, the way Kitty had once upon a time. Here's a quick *précis:* The speaker has taken a twig with leaves from a favorite, freestanding tree. He twines a little moss around it, and he keeps it within sight in his room. Whitman closes with the observation…

> *Yet it remains to me a curious token, it makes me think of*
> *manly love;*
> *For all that, and the live-oak glistens there in Louisiana*
> *solitary in a wide*
>   *flat space,*
> *Uttering joyous leaves all its life without a friend a lover near,*
> *I know very well I could not.*

It's quite the poem, methinks.

Afternoon with a Faun

If I had to do it all over again, I'd be a Broadway chorus dancer, going from show to show, from fan kicks to time steps to dream ballets, giving my all until my legs gave out.

I say this as if there had been a time when I could have become an actual chorus boy but chose instead to go into endodontics, or academia. There wasn't. By the time I realized the career existed—the night *A Chorus Line* swept the Tony Awards on ABC Television the 18th of April 1976—it was already too late for me.

I grew up in rural Nebraska, where people *farmed* for exercise. I had no upper body strength and didn't know how to acquire any. In high school, I didn't know that the jocks had a workout room all to themselves with barbells and dumbbells and weighted wall pulleys. There would have been a hate crime if I'd turned up in their secret clubhouse aiming to do some curls. My spindly, sibilant self was already a target for pink bellies, wedgies, and unkind nicknames. Cruel fate to have a first name that doubled as a British slang verb for fuck, crueler still that Janelle Weckwerth broadcast this information to all of Red Cloud Junior High. Things went further south when Lars Tadder learned from an uncle in the navy that "a jolly roger" denoted male-on-male anal intercourse. My high school yearbook is filled with inscriptions that begin with "Hey Jolly!" or "Dear Jolly Boy:"

I thank Title IX for my first dance class in high school—tap. *Anything* short of meningitis to get out of basketball. The class was seventeen girls and me, another story of my life. I wore my reversible black and gold gym shirt emblazoned with Atira the Pawnee Corn Mother (our politically insensitive school mascot), white shorts, a jockstrap, porn-star athletic knee-high socks, and black patent leather Capezios, the look more Land of Misfit Toys than Gene Kelly.

Ballet, which I started my first year at Knox College in Galesburg, Illinois, looked better on me than tap because I had amazing turnout. I had been born with a case of *metatarsus adductus* severe enough to require plaster leg casts for my first six months of life to make my bones grow in the proper direction. When the casts came off, my pigeon-toed feet, tibiae and fibulae had been over-corrected, hence my reverse foot rotation greater than 180 degrees. My mother still gets weepy to recall the sound of my legs clinking against each other while we nursed, and I have to remind her that the cramped dimensions of her womb—a leading cause of *metatarsus adductus*—had been out of her direct control. To this day, I can place my heels together and make my feet point a smidgen backwards without falling over.

For ballet, my black tights, leotard, and nude-colored dance belt had to be ordered in special from Rockford, because once again, I was the only boy. For the purposes of this story, it's essential to understand the differences between a jockstrap and a dance belt. The former has two stretchy leg straps and a mesh pouch that permits air circulation. It consolidates the junk and pushes it forward, in the way that Japanese men's briefs do today. A dance belt, on the other hand, has one cigarette-width thong strap that pulls the junk backwards, slightly upwards, and locks it there, lending the male crotch an ideal, Ken-doll smoothness. A bulge, whatever its size, is unavoidable, but legible moose knuckles are *verboten*. The three-inch, double-thick waistband of the belt also promotes line, which, as you may already know, is *everything* in ballet. Air circulation and stretch are off-mission. As is comfort, although the rigors of the barre kept me from contemplating the state of my genitals, literally sent to the back of the bus for ninety androgynous minutes two mornings a week.

I hadn't needed to see *The Red Shoes* to understand that ballet was both art and calling, one I should have begun at five. Classes ended with exhilarating diagonal runs of leaps from one corner of the girl's gymnasium to the other. Then I'd undress alone in a one-shower, three-locker alcove for boys next to the equipment room. Removing a jockstrap is a shuck and a fling. A dance belt is a peel-and-drag that invites contemplation. That first semester of freshman year, I was also taking Greek Civilization, the way one did at liberal arts colleges forty years ago, and the man-boy love crux was on the syllabus. My exertions, the setting, the privacy—not even a mirror for this North Platte Narcissus—and finally, the rush of cool air on my freshly liberated package gave me post-class erections that I would attend to then and there with thoughts of a strong, patient *erastes* strolling to the gymnasium for a workout, who then found me, an *eromenos* eager for initiation, in a steam room scented with eucalyptus and rosemary. I've never tracked the exact location for my daddy fixation, but college ballet class is one of the placeholders. Rinsing the semen from my chest in the shower, I'd clock the canister of Right Guard in my gym bag on the bench. If not yet a man in age or psychology, I was male again.

Jazz came after tap and ballet. I spent the summer as a rising college sophomore doing musicals with the Soangetaha Players, a mix of non-pro community stalwarts and Knox students. Summer stock was important to my education; I first experienced the rush of live performance, and I met my first out gay men (okay, out-ish, this being Western Illinois during the Jimmy Carter Administration). I slept with two of them. Derek, the second, confirmed one morning on his futon, that waist-up, I had the body of a fifteen-year old. It was an observation, not a criticism.

Waist-down, my body was age-appropriate, with long, strong legs and, as we know, great turnout. Candy Wadley, resident SP choreographer (and Mary Kay saleswoman), discovered my talent for rapid pelvic undulation, which we exploited for my slutty turns as Kit Kat Boy #3 in *Cabaret* and, although hardly the butchest Muleteer in *Man of La Mancha,* I learned offstage how to make the actress playing Dulcinea/Aldonza laugh, such that she would wink at me onstage when I pressed her left boob in "The Abduction." By August, the company had grown tight enough to go naked behind a scrim at the end of "Where Do I Go?" in *Hair,* but the top brass at Soangetaha—pillars of Galesburg society—threatened to close us before we opened. Today we'd certainly be canceled, not for those five measures of hazy, backlit nudity, but for the slanted eye makeup and pan-Asian accents we had blithely adopted for *Flower Drum Song.*

Also essential that summer was meeting David Towle, who, forty years on, remains my dearest friend. He played clarinet in the SP orchestra. Unlike me, he was too Catholic to act on his queerness. We roomed together sophomore year and followed a trail of gay breadcrumbs...Lily Tomlin leading to Bette Midler, then back to Ruth Draper; Whitman and Beardsley and Wilde, to Burroughs and Renault; *Of Human Bondage* to *Now, Voyager* to *All About Eve*—enough said. When David, an art history major, applied for a semester in Rome, I copied the move and applied for a semester in Paris. I had been waffling between economics and English as my major, but with seven years of French and a decent ear and accent, how much could go wrong during a twenty-week commitment? I did screw up on the fine print—David would be in Italy in the fall, while my program was spring only, such that we wouldn't overlap and be able to Fodor-backpack-blitzkrieg the rest of Europe.

*

During our second Soangetaha summer, you could say I had my first (clandestine) relationship, with Cam Kreidler, a pharmacist on the Chamber of Commerce whose wife was also in the company. Things got ugly when Joanie Kreidler found out. She tripped me onstage one night in *Li'l Abner,* and I had to get four stitches for a split chin. Knox College, acting *in loco parentis,* managed to keep the court documents sealed when Joanie sued for divorce, but everyone in Galesburg seemed to know that I was the almost underage alienator of Cam's affections, a wicked faun who wound up shouldering the stag's share of the moral opprobrium. How was it *my* fault that Cam had been an emotional virgin with men until me? How was it *my* fault that he and Joanie hadn't gotten their shit together after ten years of wedlock? It seemed a clear case of blaming and shaming the victim.

Junior year, what with David already in Florence, and Cam assuming we were going to live on love in an apartment over his drugstore, Paris couldn't come soon enough. Fortunately, Cam's lawyer called a halt to any meetings between us until the separation agreement was filed. I didn't even say goodbye.

There would be no jazz hands in Paris, a dance form then unknown to the French, but included in my semester abroad paperwork was a list of performance *ateliers.* The *Schola Cantorum de Paris* on the rue St.

Jacques, close to my *chambre de bonne*, offered ballet. I had no idea at the time of Schola Cantorum's cultural significance. Founded in 1894 as an independent rival to the Conservatoire de Paris, its roster of teaching artists and alumni included Satie, Milhaud, Varèse, Landowska, d'Indy, Messiaen, and Cole Porter. The 17th century building had been constructed for English Benedictine monks fleeing the religious wars at home and was later used as a detention house under Robespierre's Reign of Terror.

As someone who likes to test well, I enrolled at the beginner's level, even after two years of ballet at Knox. Sessions were structured similarly; my *ronds de jambe* and *pas de chat* certainly felt more classical in a mirrored salon that had served as a reception room for James II, the final Catholic monarch of England. The most historic structure I'd ever been in was Abraham Lincoln's House in Springfield—and that had all been roped off.

This time there were other men in class, swarthy stalks whose upper body strength prompted wishful thoughts of a Franco-Hellenic Sacred Band of Thebes grinding it out in a post-class orgy, but there were no showers or locker room at the Schola that I was ever able to locate. We'd drop our street clothes and bags behind the piano and move noiselessly to the barre. Afterwards, I'd rush home and climb six flights to relieve my horny self in my *chambre de bonne*.

As the literature warned, making French friends was tough. The natives weren't prone to small talk, even were I capable of it, so in the end, I didn't attempt connections. Sex with strangers would be good language practice, but if there was a bustling *quartier gai,* I didn't find that either. With so much to do and see and absorb, I can't say I felt lonely. Having David Towle around would have been a plus, but I reasoned that we would always have Paris.

Besides taste-testing pastry (two every afternoon), my favorite activity was being an *assistant de première langue vivante* at *Collège Raymond Queneau* in the 5th arrondissement. The first teaching I ever did was holding twice-weekly conversations with fourteen-year-olds hungry for American slang. It was a free lunch, with wine, and Marie-Laure, the regular instructor, grateful for the break in her schedule, let me follow my muse. I taught the kids to sing "Frankie and Johnny" and "Disco

Duck." We analyzed the lyrics to "Eleanor Rigby." One gorgeous April afternoon, just as the chestnut trees had begun to bloom, we walked to the Jardin de Luxembourg, where I taught them a dance combination, hitch kicks and all, that I'd performed as a cowhand in the Soangetaha *Oklahoma!*. I was proud that we drew a crowd.

I envied the hand-holds and butt slaps among the boys, impossible in America, and I didn't discourage the girls who crushed on me. In return, the students traded their slang with me, and taught me Gallic foodways. A baguette is torn, not sliced. Hands above the table *always*; the hand below is assumed to be roaming a neighbor's lap. I won't forget the uproar I caused when asked about my lunch and I replied, "Je suis plein," which meant that I was pregnant, rather than full. You insult your hosts when you tell them that a particular dish or meal was "good/ excellent/delicious/wonderful." Of course it was; compliments of that sort went *without* saying. Thierry, a child of divorce, taught me that brie is to be sliced along the diagonal. His French grandparents had never accepted the way his American father, now exiled to Texas, would cut the nose off a slab of brie.

I was touched when Ghislaine Laroque, the English chair at *Collège Queneau,* told me that my band of *quatrièmes* had insisted I accompany them on their field trip to Mont St. Michel. I'd only a month left in Paris; transit strikes had twice derailed my plan to visit Versailles and Chartres.

If you've been, you know the worth of a trip to Mont St. Michel. In terms of age, the only comparable site in North America are the remains of the pre-Columbian city of Cahokia, 120 earthen mounds just north of St. Louis erected by early members of the Illini Confederation. Undifferentiated grassy elevations with concrete staircases versus Gothic buttresses and a drawbridge wheel? Both attractions are UNESCO World Heritage Sites, but there was no comparison for me between Cahokia and Mont St. Michel. Sighting the spires of the five-tiered tidal island that pierced the clouds on the long approach, I thought, and not for the first time that spring, "Here is the point of Europe."

I spent the day in a daze, lighting three-franc candles at every shrine in the cathedral, pressing my hands against plaster and stone and iron until I had to wash them before lunch. The kids were less impressed. Paris had outlawed skyscrapers after the scandalous erection of the Tour

Montparnasse in 1973, so I suppose a trip to Chicago might have excited them in the same way I felt that day, but, again, the Sears Tower versus a medieval abbey? *La Belle France* wins in a landslide.

Paris to Mont St. Michel takes four and a half hours, but it's a global travel axiom that the field trip bus will always be late. So it was for our return leg. Ghislaine placed witchy calls to the tour company, but that was all that could be done. Afternoon stretched to evening in a world before smartphones. Ghislaine, Marie-Laure, fifteen pupils, and I waited for our driver and watched the party lights of the souvenir shops and *crêperies* blink off one by one. Mont St. Michel is celebrated for its high tides, but we had missed its first appearance that morning, and hopefully wouldn't still be stuck—and starved—for its return around 9:30 pm. A student had brought a deck of cards, but we soon ran out of energy and light enough even to manage a game of Go Fish, for which I've forgotten the translation.

With our coats and jackets in the bus, no one was dressed for the maritime chill. Eventually, we formed a tight, seated circle around a grate that provided random blasts of steam. (Ghislaine and Marie-Laure ignored the two couples making their own heat in stone niches older than Charlemagne.) I taught everyone English expressions for the cold. Once the group had grasped what a brass monkey's balls were, and a witch's teat, and a well-digger's backside, and Hell with the furnace turned off, etc., *and* learned how to pronounce the words intelligibly (the French don't care how badly their accents sound) I strung them into a ditty. Thierry, sitting to my left, provided off-color hand gestures. Then we all stood and made a dance to go along with the tune, singing louder and faster, and finally generating a little heat with our kicks and hand jive. It wasn't Maria guiding the Von Trapp children through the solfège scale, but the composition and performance of "Codor Zan" ("Colder Than") was a first teaching moment to call my own.

When the driver turned up, reeking of calvados, Ghislaine and Marie-Laure scoured his ears with ribbons of French so salty the students stepped into the bus as if it were the tumbrel to the guillotine. Thierry grabbed the seat next to mine. He had no coat, so I lent him my windbreaker; inadequate relief, so I put my arm around him and pressed my fingers up and down his arm and shoulder until the heating kicked in and he stopped shivering.

He waited until it was dark to tell me how much he missed his father, whom he was going to visit that summer. He asked whether Nebraska was close to Houston. He asked if he could meet up with me in America. To be kind, I said it wasn't out of the question. His head dropped to my shoulder as he fell asleep. At some point, he curled his left hand into my right, on top of my leg. I listened to the peaceful chuff of his breaths on my collarbone. His trust was overwhelming. I think only the driver and I stayed awake for the entire ride. Thierry was fourteen, and I was twenty, and this was the most tender experience of my life.

I was groggy for ballet the next morning but rallied. After months of cheese, *charcuterie,* and a couple hundred *délices de pâtissier*, I had gained at least ten pounds, so dragging my dance belt down my hips and thighs had become something of a challenge. While attending to my customary need after ballet, thoughts of Thierry entered my mind—the pale brown brushes of hair at the edges of his upper lip, his botched attempts at an American "g" when saying "Roger," his lewd gesture for a well-digger's backside in the 'Codor Zan' dance, the smell of his hair against my cheek in the dark bus. Then, more explicit images. For the first time in my life, I was the *erastes*, and Thierry was my *eromenos*.

Degrading Thierry's trust this way was immediate. Five minutes after climaxing, I stood to grab a towel from the door hook for a shower down the hall and noticed that my penis had assumed terrifying contours. It had not drained completely. The blood was backed up in a stiff, mottled collar just below the glans, which had darkened in color from the pressure. It resembled a club on a playing card. Stifling a scream, I looked up the French in my *Harrap's Collegiate Dictionary*—*le trèfle*, the club suit. I stopped pacing to gently, then violently, shake its stem. There was no pain. There was no change.

I could only theorize that the release of the extra-tight dance belt, followed by an ultra-fast toss-off, had altered the circulation in my groin. Would it grow black and fall off? Would this be permanent? I threw on some clothes, sped down six flights, and chose a first solution: in full defiance of the French edicts against snacking *and* against eating on the street, I bought and ate a chocolate éclair, a mocha *religieuse*, and a shortbread *sablé*. I circled the block, but there were no *pissoirs* where I could check my status. I re-mounted the stairs of my building with a slow, entirely counterfeit balletic poise, hoping that leg movement and the sugar and fat rush to my stomach would drain the blood from my Ace of Clubs.

No change. I tore through my papers, looking for the phone number of L'Hôpital Américain in Neuilly. I raced to a pay phone on the street and babbled about "un pénis qui ressemble tout d'un coup à un trèfle" to a receptionist. She didn't understand—and how was it that the first line of defense at the *American* Hospital *didn't* speak English?—until my panicked repetitions of "Ça ne se dégonfle pas!" ("It won't deflate!") broke through the language barrier, and she suggested the emergency room.

I had no money for a taxi. The *trajet en métro,* burned in my memory, was Odéon to Réaumur-Sébastopol to Louise Michel. Unsure of how to protect my junk in the subway car, or promote its recovery, I alternated sitting and standing, counting stops, praying and vowing to light candles for a host of Christian saints and martyrs, begging God for His forgiveness. I scrolled back to the time before my penis had taken on such importance—thirteen, a year younger than Thierry, a year before I became Jolly Roger—then imagined my life to come if my club dropped permanently from its stem, fitting punishment for having entertained sexual thoughts about a teenager. Outside of Attic Greece, the *erastes* is a child molester. A flash to Cam Kreidler added "homewrecker" to my list of sins. I did the math, but the greater age difference between me and Cam, than between me and Thierry, actually made me feel worse. I could have been kinder to Cam, said goodbye for starters, sent a postcard, for fuck's sake! The four stitches in my chin from Joanie Kreidler's wrath seemed trifling next to the present crisis in my undershorts. Nor had I ever given a second's thought to Joanie's feelings. I'd blow out of Galesburg in a year. She was a townie alone with her wedding album. *She* was the injured party. I thanked God that there were no little Kreidlers; I even prayed for their reconciliation.

From the subway to Avenue Victor Hugo, then a right turn to the hospital, was a ten-minute sprint. Registration was swift; the *précis* of my case drew no comment from the staff, and when I finally had a moment, I ran to check my condition in a toilet stall.

Things were well on their way to normal.

Had I overreacted?

By the time I saw the attending, an Italian with no English, I had to draw a picture on his prescription pad to help him comprehend what had happened to my penis, because now "Il s'était completèment dégonflé." As a gesture of prudence, and because clearly, I was an insane person, he produced a wand, which I now recognize was a primitive ultrasound transducer, and ran it over and around my organ. His conclusion: "Aucune trace de dérangement physique, Monsieur Hauf." My youth, I think, led him to suggest, as parting advice, that I engage in more frequent acts of masturbation.

The morning after my special afternoon at the American Hospital, I rang up Ghislaine Laroque at the *Collége Queneau.* I was afraid that the sight of Thierry might knot my mind again, if not my body. I preferred to remember his eagerness in claiming the seat beside me, and the reluctance I had read in his features when he returned my windbreaker, and so I said to Ghislaine, regretfully, that I wouldn't be able to finish out the semester with the *quatrièmes.*

Ballet class was easier to quit; I was but a momentary glyph against three centuries of human indifference captured in the mirrored *salon* of the Scuola Cantorum, and let's face it, my upper body had not been built to match my legs. Two days before my flight home, a hospital bill came in the mail. Semi-socialized healthcare had reduced my *grande maladie*— or was it a phantom affliction?—to a pittance, but I made France pick up that check.

Medically induced erections of five hours or more are currently the stuff of late-night drug warnings and prime-time comedy. My brand of urogenital-circulatory distress has not been described in any literature I've ever been able to find, nor have my doctor friends, one of whom spent thirty years in emergency medicine, ever observed the condition in a patient. Increasing openness in the non-cis and transgender communities has introduced the idea of "tucking" devices to mainstream America. Men in ballet, however, must still make their peace with the dance belt, the fit of which, I learned once upon a time, should be snug, but not tight.

I also recently read where the French are finally getting serious about raising the age of legal consent to fifteen. I'm for that too.

Who Are Your People?

Trip Buttenwieser and I were standing on the corner of Park and Chapel when he handed me a fuzzy beige box.

"What is this?" I asked.

"Open it and find out," he said.

It was a small gold ring about a quarter inch in width.

"What's it for?"

"Your pinkie."

Trip and I had had three dates. No one had ever given me a piece of jewelry. Gangsters wore pinkie rings. The box yawned on my palm.

"What does it mean?" I asked at last.

"It means I'm way into you, Roger."

I didn't know how to answer that, so Trip took the ring from the box and pushed it down my right pinkie. It fit. "How did you know what size to get?"

"I checked your hand against mine while you were asleep."

"Why the right hand?"

"It's the gay side."

"Uh-huh," I said, clocking the sidewalk to see if anyone could hear.

"It's our one-week anniversary, Roger," he said and, before I could back away, he kissed me right in front of Gag Jr's, a lunch counter that I hoped wasn't full of construction workers on break. "Happy Anniversary," I said through pressed lips.

Gay men weren't that out in 1985 in New Haven, Connecticut, but Trip Buttenwieser was a bold one, and big with the gifts. He next redressed my lack of a leather coat. The week before Thanksgiving, a box from Bergdorf-Goodman arrived bearing not a black motorcycle jacket, but a dark brown, hooded suede parka, whose drawstring waist and caramel kidskin accents appliquéd to its amplified shoulders mark it as a garment of its moment. I was not averse to being trendy, so I enjoyed wearing Trip's gift, although my roommate, David, and I secretly called the coat "Miss Thing." When I told David that the Buttenwiesers celebrated Hanukah *and* Christmas, he began to sing "Santa Baby" in Trip's presence, and told him that his next big gesture should be a car. Trip, pleased to be cast as Lord Bountiful, didn't understand he was being mocked.

They were oil and water. Trip's terrible mistake the first morning he woke up in our apartment was to say to David, *en route* to Mass, that Roman Catholics, as a class, were low-class. David Towle, a scholar of the Italian Baroque, could have countered with a list of two hundred masterpieces in marble, charcoal, oil, *terra cotta* and *terza rima,* but chose instead to turn the other cheek and fume about Trip's slur to his people until he left for Naples on a Kress Fellowship in April. I believe we were all counting the days for that.

David passed no remarks about Trip's people, because Trip had gotten there first. He was the first person to detail for me the markers that differentiated German Jews from Russian Jews. The Buttenwiesers hadn't escaped the *shtetl;* they had emigrated from Lübeck in the mid-19th century and settled in New York City as part of "Our Crowd." Trip's sisters, Eileen and Grace Buttenwieser, owed their Anglo-ish given names to six generations of assimilation. Trip was born Ross Gerald Buttenwieser III. As an early example of what I classified as "Salisbury Knowledge" (Trip had boarded at the all-male Salisbury School), he explained on our first date, with a false humility I found endearing, that boys who were born "the Thirds" would choose among Terry, Tray, or Trip as nicknames; all derived from *"tertius,"* Latin for "three." I might have responded with the question, "Why Trip over Terry or Tray (or Ross)"? but instead felt a need to translate my last name, Hauf, into English. It means "pile" or "heap." As in *der Dreckhauf*—"heap of dirt," or colloquially, "pile of shit." The exchange was an early example of a dynamic in our relationship: when Trip went high, I'd go low.

Trip's humility was false, because having shared the stage with him, I knew when he was acting. That first date had taken place two days after our show, an Edward Gorey potpourri called *Gorey Stories,* closed a

Halloween weekend run at the Yale Cabaret. I had played Little Henry, and Trip had been Jasper Ankle. In our backstage energy circle before every performance, I'd given his right hand an extra squeeze with my left (as well as the left hand of Beverly Michnewicz with my right). I vaguely sensed that Trip had tried to chat me up in rehearsals, but embarrassment kept me from social interaction. Trip and the rest of the company were students at the Yale School of Drama, the launch for, among many others, Henry Winkler, Meryl Streep, Sigourney Weaver, Frances McDormand, Paul Giamatti, and Lupita Nyong'o, while I, a Yale library employee, was, as the saying goes, punching above my weight, only cast at the Cabaret as a Little Henry replacement last-minute. At that point, any warm body would do.

That was me, warm body and recent theater star of tiny Knox College in Galesburg, Illinois, now spinning his wheels in New Haven. Too afraid to apply to MFA programs, or to move to New York, I'd followed David and his free ride with the Yale History of Art Department. Were a knife at my throat, I'd announce that my goal was to be a professional actor, but my chickenshit true self knew better. *Gorey Stories* had been a fine abstract notion, but among the exalted drama students, I was emotionally frozen. In front of an audience, I felt grotesquely self-conscious. The pre-show hand squeeze with Trip and Beverly had been my freest choice.

Trip wouldn't say as much on our first date. He had learned that he didn't have the talent to become a successful actor, and so had enrolled at the drama school as a theater management student. *Gorey Stories* had been a lark. His biggest credit had been as a chorus swing on a national tour of *Sugar Babies*, a fact that impressed me until he revealed that a first cousin was the lead producer. When Trip leaned in for a goodbye at my apartment door, I countered with some honesty of my own. I confessed that I had had not one, but *two* sex dreams about him in the past week.

"So, what are we waiting for?" he asked.

"A second date," I stammered, unable to meet his eyes.

Three days later, we hit the hay between the steak and the lemon mousse he'd made. In another five days, the pinkie ring.

✳

Trip Buttenwieser had a coating of body hair that made it easy to accept the *Esquire* cliché that a man-pelt signaled extra testosterone. At twenty-seven, he knew where he was going—he wanted to be a Broadway producer—and he had the drive to get there. On his arm, wearing Miss Thing, I felt not unlike a chorine or a gun moll.

Having Trip on my side at night helped insulate me from my dreary daytimes. When I thought too much about my job, its Sisyphean nature would put me in a panic. I was an entry-level sorter in the cataloguing division at Sterling Memorial Library. Forty hours a week, I carted books and periodicals from the loading dock to different department stations in a cavern that students and faculty never saw. Its stained-glass windows fronted York Street like the rest of its neo-Gothic neighbors, but this was Yale scripted by Kafka. The overheated workplace smelled like B.O. I learned where and when to hold my breath. There were so many withered limbs in cataloguing, I visualized a *Yale Daily News* classified ad from the fifties that read, "Licked Polio? You've got a job!" Unloading my wares for an army of eye patches and coke-bottle glasses, prostheses, morbid obesities, harelips, hemangiomas, goiters, buzzing ear transistors, and a glossary of skin conditions, I felt like Walt Whitman nursing Union soldiers at the Sheridan Street Hospital.

My mistake one morning was to ask Olive McFadden, whose tiny figure and spinal curvature made her the "Bent Sparrow of Anthropology," how things were going. Olive, proudly in place since 1933, gestured to the stalagmites of moldering backlog around her and said, almost blithely, it sounded to me, that she was only two years behind schedule.

Pre-vomit salivation gathered in my throat. A job where you would never ever *ever* catch up? Forget Nurse Whitman—I was Old Scratch delivering a daily dose of brimstone. Most of the cataloguers belonged to Local 34; I began to daydream of insurrection, but who was our common oppressor? The Yale Corporation? Melville Dewey? Johannes Gutenberg?

"At least you're working with smart people," said my mother when I griped about work in a phone call home.

Occasionally, I would spot cataloguers outdoors, and they would seem indistinguishable from the panhandlers who worked the students on Whitney Avenue or stood in line for soup at the side door of Trinity Church on the Green. They were like the unhoused population, with purses and briefcases instead of overstuffed Macy's bags. What had happened to them on the fateful days that they decided that a permanent position in the butt end of Sterling was a positive life choice? How many days, weeks, or months might I be from a similar decision? For now, I felt that as long as the wheels on my cart ran true, I couldn't be pushed to rot behind one of those desks.

If this ugly riff about my workplace—of which I am presently ashamed—was my audition piece at the Buttenwiesers' Thanksgiving in Stony Creek, then I killed it. Eileen and Grace laughed their heads off, and although Ross Gerald *secundus* merely acknowledged that humor was happening in his vicinity, Trip's mother, Florence, blotted tears of mirth with a cream and écru linen napkin. (Mothers are the test.) Trip, who had yet to hear this side of me, beamed, drew my hand from my plate, and covered it with kisses. I knew what he was thinking. Watch out—he bites. Little Henry was more than just a pretty face.

Trip was the baby and the prince; even at that first holiday meal, I could tell that his sisters resented him, Eileen, for example, insisting that I be shown his last actor's headshot. That it was ready to hand in the top drawer of Florence's writing desk prompted an eye roll between the sisters.

"I don't miss it," I said loyally, referring to his hair in the photo. "He's cute no matter what."

"Thanks, babe," said Trip, this time finding my face with his lips. PDAs, even *en famille,* made me uneasy. I wasn't yet out to my parents, and any one of us might be carrying the virus, for which there was no treatment. Were Trip's parents reconciled to there being no Ross Walter *quartus*?

"Where are you keeping your rug these days?" asked Grace.

"It's an interesting auburn shade," said Eileen to me.

"It's at my apartment," Trip said, with an edge, then, trying to lighten things up, said he felt its color was closer to ranch mink. That drew in Secundus, who remembered it costing about as much as Flo's mink jacket, he'd written the check, leading Trip to recall that he'd retired that loan in full, and that Dad had refused to accept interest, but he'd be happy to pay him eight percent now just to shut down the topic of his rug—a legitimate deductible expense for a working actor—once and for all time. The sisters, meanwhile, were batting the figure of eight percent back and forth like a shuttlecock, leaving Florence and me to share a smile that somehow acknowledged that money was vulgar and families were impossible. She and Trip had the same button nose. I decided I liked her. Or decided to like her.

When silence prevailed, Florence asked Trip when he was going to take me to New York to meet Till and Ben.

"I thought I'd wait until their holiday windows are up," he replied.

"That will be a great treat," she said to me. "They will just love you, Roger."

(At this, another side-eye from the cashmere barracudas.)

❋

Till was not short for Matilda. Till was Gough Thompson Tilghman, a long-limbed scion of the Chesapeake, tan and lean from sailing and tennis, with great teeth and an appealing reserve. His partner, Benjamin Sachsen, a Charlestonian cousin to Secundus Buttenwieser, was a stubby, loquacious butterball whose chief conversational interest was genealogies. Partially deaf, Ben didn't know his voice carried. "Who are his people?" he asked Trip in a Foghorn Leghorn accent not five minutes after we'd shaken a first December snow from our boots inside their antique shop on Madison Avenue, meaning *my* people. I wasn't supposed to have overheard him, so any retort from my piehole, which would have involved a truck stop and home detention (sarcasm being my first defense at twenty-three), had to be stifled.

I let it go then, but pressed Trip on the milk train back to New Haven for his answer.

"I told Ben that that stuff wasn't important," he said. He'd put his gloved fingertips between mine, like a lattice.

I didn't believe him. "No really, Trip. What did you tell him?"

"I said you came from a family of Midwestern academics."

"Great Plains," I said, ribbing him. "There's a distinction." (Like German v. Russian Jews.) My people had settled in Nebraska, raising themselves from wheat farming to blacksmithing to gas station franchises to town governance to, in the case of my parents, state school professorships.

Till had rowed for Harvard, and Ben had been "the only unashamed dicksmoker" his year at Amherst. Their thirty-three years as a couple staggered me, as had the treasures in their shop—Baccarat and Cartier, Tartanware, Meissen monkey figurines, cloisonné casket boxes. They'd been, as Florence promised, a total treat.

"Every family has funny uncles," I said to Trip in the train, "but gay people don't have people *per se*, since we don't reproduce."

"Let's be our own people then," said Trip with a smile. His thought felt so in tune with the embrace extended to us by a couple who'd found each other in the Korean War I draped my scarf over his trousers, removed my glove, unzipped him, and got busy. The nearest passenger was snoozing four rows away. Like I said, he'd go high, then I'd go low.

I may have been a commoner, but my mother had dinged the importance of bread-and-butter notes into me. (Perhaps they're a snippet of gay boy DNA, like Christmas crèches, *petits fours,* and a soft spot for Lovey Howell.) Whether nurture or nature, my first formal thank-you to Till and Ben earned a rave in a phone call to Trip and an invitation for a New Year's weekend at their country house in Bucks County.

We would borrow Secundus' Porsche and avoid Manhattan by crossing the Tappan Zee Bridge in Tarrytown. We overpacked our nicest things. Trip had bought me a leather weekend bag for Christmas with secret zipped compartments. Into one of them, like a bride with trousseau lingerie, I slipped two pairs of *French* boxer shorts I'd blown my holiday paycheck on. I had given Trip an Art Deco silver and onyx brooch from my favorite antiques store on Upper State Street.

The weekend involved liberal doses of Tilghman eggnog, a family recipe that involved four different brown spirits. It was said that Lt. Colonel Tench Tilghman made the eggnog for his boss, General George

Washington, before the Battle of Monmouth in 1778. Till explained that the alcohol cooked the eggs and the cream, so refrigeration was unnecessary.

For his part, Ben outlined the histories of both the Sachsens and the Buttenwiesers, who, like many families in the Southern Jewish diaspora, had begun with an eponymous dry goods store on Main Street, then went on to help found or fund hospitals, refugee societies, Hadassah chapters, regional orchestras, and college scholarships. Helping Ben lay the table for dinner, I was introduced to the seven kinds of fork: dinner, fish, fruit cocktail, ice cream, luncheon, oyster, and salad. Then, we moved on to the serving pieces. Ben explained how specialized flatware took the place of television in the 19th century. The effects of the potent eggnog, the elegance of the furnishings, wall hangings, and *objets*, a crackling fire in the hearth, Sarah Vaughan on the turntable, 1986 in the offing, Ben's comic monologue while our partners cooked, made me feel happy in a way I'd never experienced. The nonpareil feeling of safety and contentment accounts for why, to this day, I can still distinguish a buckwheat cake server from a tomato lift.

It snowed the following night, New Year's Eve, over seven courses at the Lambertville Station restaurant. There were many toasts, we to them, they to us, to Buttenwiesers great and small, to gay rights, to *The New York Times,* and even to Reaganomics, Till explaining that their shop had enjoyed its best year ever.

During dessert, Ben, wanting to know how the plague affected our life between the sheets, brought up the Princeton Rub, an unfamiliar term he delighted in explaining.

"It's phallic *outer*course. You achieve satisfaction via friction between your hangdown, and your partner's stomach, thighs, natal cleft, or axilla, that is to say, the pit of the arm, or arm*pit*."

"Oh, you mean intercrural, I said, lowering my voice in an attempt to set a volume level for Ben. "*Frottage.*"

"You can be French about it, Roger, if you like," he replied, "but they say Jimmy Stewart invented it at Princeton in 1932."

I began to blush. Trip and I hadn't discussed it, but I missed unsafe sex. I suspect my two dreams about him were hotter than what we managed to accomplish together. We weren't so paranoid as to forgo kissing, but fellatio through condoms was way too much effort. Mostly, we traded hand jobs. From time to time, we did the Princeton Rub, Trip gaining more from the technique than I ever could. I chalked that up to his years in an all-male boarding school.

Finally, Trip said, "We do everything we can, Ben. Thanks for asking."

"How about those dental dams the lesbians use?" His voice was now loud enough to attract the attention of the busboys clearing tables. "I made a sales associate at Rexall Drugs open a package and show me one. I never saw anything so ridiculous in my life. How are you supposed to eat pussy through a rubber cocktail napkin?"

Ben's merry fist to the table drew the *maître d'*, and Till asked for the check.

Later, in bed, the snow gathering softly on the windowsills, Trip and I laughed that really, there was no such thing as a free dinner. We held hands under the covers as we drifted off, me hoping that one day we might have all that Ben and Till possessed, Trip plotting how to go about it.

In March, a crisis: Sterling Library offered me a permanent cataloguing position. If I said no, would I feel the fool for refusing to step onto the first American ladder lowered my way? If I said yes, would that mean I was giving up on life? Trip stopped my dithering by making an appointment with sister Grace, who was a job placement counselor for mentally impaired young adults. I met her at her office just west of the New Haven Green. Her wall posters paired natural vistas with motivating captions. A framed photo of the teenaged Buttenwiesers stood on her desk, Trip with a head of tight, dark curls.

"Congratulations on your job offer," she began.

"Oy," was all I could muster in response.

I couldn't tell if she was more or less terrifying without Eileen beside her.

"What are you good at, Roger?"

"Listening?" I said, attempting breeze.

"That I do know," she replied. Trip and I had dinner every other Saturday in Stony Creek. He and Florence did the cooking, and I played court jester/tension breaker to the rest.

"I write a mean bread and butter note."

Grace's lips stretched into a facsimile of a smile. "Did you like your Valentine's Day present?"

"Honestly," I sighed. "I tried to talk your brother out of it."

Trip had had notecards engraved for me at Crane's. Knowing by now I didn't like extravagant purchases I could never reciprocate, he assured me that once the *Roger Hale Hauf* template had been created, it could be re-used—with an economy of scale—for any and all other forms of stationery I might wish to acquire.

"He's big with the gifts," Grace said. "At least this time, he didn't have your names engraved together."

"Together?"

As far as I knew, Trip had never had another serious boyfriend, not that I would have cared, except that Grace was clearly baiting me.

"Ross Gerald Buttenwieser III eats up a lot of paper," I said. "Whose name did he engrave with his last time?"

She tucked a stray curl behind her ear, then folded her hands on her blotter.

"Trip didn't mention Elayne Colton?"

Falsely chagrined at having let something slip, Grace declared the story wasn't hers to share. We held our gazes for a moment—I was having none of that. Eventually, she stood behind her desk and motioned, as she would with her other jittery clients, for me to join her on the sofa.

Elayne Colton was the little sister of Grace's college friend, Heidi. She and Trip had met at Heidi's graduation party from Mt. Holyoke a week after the *Sugar Babies* tour had ended. He and Elayne had fallen in love and divided that summer between Stony Creek and the Colton compound in Westport. Renting a suite at the Plaza for the occasion, Trip proposed marriage, even though Elayne had a final year left at Bowdoin. Ignoring the advice of both sets of parents, they set a date in December, issued invitations, created a registry at Tiffany's, and held tastings with every caterer in Fairfield County.

The stationery wardrobe he had ordered for *Elayne Alice Colton Buttenwieser* included jaunty *Elayne & Trip* half-sheets with pistachio envelope liners. This was a final red flag for the bride, who cancelled the wedding three days before the ceremony. There was no scandal, Grace explained. Elayne had merely had an attack of common sense. The most she would ever say on the subject was that Trip had made it difficult for her to breathe.

The release of the Elayne Colton missile tabled further talk of my employment opportunities. In the end, I got a new job the "Our Crowd" way: Grace called Secundus and told him to call in a favor from his college buddy, the grandson of the founder of Enson's Menswear on Chapel Street. I left Sterling Library, started in shoes, and, surprising even myself, proved an adept salesman with a flair for customer service. It was better money.

✳

My feelings about Trip's broken engagement were confused. Although no one knew any, bisexuals were said to walk the earth. (The fluidity of gender identities and sexual preferences we enjoy today was decades away.) I suppose Trip's full-court press on a rising college senior could be considered embarrassing, but as far as I was concerned, post-Elayne, Trip was acting on his truer self, a positive step.

David, anxious about handing me off, made a diagnosis in our last heart-to-heart before he left for Naples. We were moving his belongings into a storage unit, a decision made after Trip broke his own lease to move in with me.

"Trip doesn't want to be gay," said David.

"He's hiding it pretty well, I said.

David scoffed. "But if fate and biology have made him gay, then he's going to be gay writ XXL. You've been swept into his tornado to become the second Mrs. Buttenwieser."

"You just hate him, that's all."

"He's a greedy, entitled pig, but—lucky for you—he's on your side."

"He should be on my side. He's my boyfriend."

End of subject. Stacking absurdly heavy boxes of art catalogues, David said he wished he had the money to spare for a second plane ticket to Italy, and I snapped that I was tired of people paying for me.

✳

My broaching the topic of Elayne Colton was, for Trip, "an ambush." We'd set off in the Porsche for a second Ben and Till weekend in Bucks County, enjoying our positions as the younger pair of an accomplished male foursome. David's verdict had stuck with me as I watched Trip fill my apartment with pots, pans, and plans. Since he did the shopping and the cooking and the cleaning and the laundry, I couldn't be Mrs. Buttenwieser. At most, I was Lovey Howell.

In New Jersey, the billboards for Flemington Furs were a fresh threat to my sense of sovereignty. I reasoned that not only would Trip want a fur coat, he would buy me one too. To head this off, I joked that no matter how successful he became in the future, if we were still together, fur coats were verboten, Miss Thing was plenty enough.

"Who is Miss Thing?" he asked.

Oops. "That's David's nickname for the coat you bought me in November," I replied, throwing my best friend under the bus.

"Goombah asshole," said Trip under his breath. "No man will ever buy him a coat."

"I don't think he wants one," I sniped.

We began arguing about my disinterest in having a future to call my own, and Trip was vexed by my floating the notion that we might not always be together. I took Mel Tormé's cover of Cole Porter's "So in Love" on the radio as my cue and asked him if Elayne Colton had allowed him boys on the side—as Linda Porter had with Cole—would he have married her?

Trip's pop-eyed take would have gotten a laugh in *Gorey Stories*. He jumped over the "Who told you?" beat to declare, "Elayne ended things, not me."

"But if she hadn't broken the engagement, would you still be married?"

"It was a rough time for me, Roger. The tour was over. I wasn't an actor. I didn't know what to do next. I didn't want to be gay. Elayne felt like a lifeline."

"That's not what I asked you. Would you still be married—with boys on the side?"

"That's not a fair question."

We sat in silence the rest of the way to Ben and Till's house, set now in a springtime collar of forsythia. On the flagstone, I thrust our hostess gift into Ben's hands.

"I suppose you were invited to Trip and Elayne's wedding," I said.

Ben betrayed no surprise at my opener. "Elayne was a lovely girl from a fine family, but we weren't asked to attend the ceremony."

"You weren't *invited*?"

"I'm not sure Flo and Ross would have approved of our attendance. We sent two place settings."

Florence had pushed Ben and Till on me as a "treat" not five months before, but hadn't asked them to Trip's wedding?

Trip looked stricken. Ben took the weekender from his hands and said that everyone made youthful mistakes. Did he mean the engagement or the ostracism?

The mood improved enough after gimlets for Trip to announce that he had landed a summer internship with the Nederlander Organization. He would work assisting their marketing efforts for the Broadway musical revival of *Me and My Girl*, which began previews on August 1st. We'd all go to opening night together just after Labor Day.

Aware in advance of Trip's big news, Ben and Till offered me, over dinner, a position in their shop. They had begun to hear the siren call of retirement. Under their training, I could learn the antiques biz top to bottom, refine my eye at trade fairs, and accompany them on buying trips. Trip and I could find a sublet that summer, and I could stay in New York and work while Trip finished drama school.

Our future was solved until Ben mentioned that one of my duties would be to clear their doorway every morning of any people who had slept there overnight, as well as keep panhandler watch during the day.

Street mendicants had become a huge problem, especially in the colder months.

"I don't think I can do that," I said. "I mean, what if they don't go?"

"Then you call the police," said Till. "They respond. Eventually."

"But they have a right to be there," I said.

"They absolutely do not have a right to be there," said Ben. "Not only do they degrade our property with their presence, they frighten customers away with their demands for money."

"Do you and Till own the sidewalk in front of the shop?" This was a genuine question.

Till narrowed his eyes. "No. The sidewalks are municipal property."

"Where are they supposed to go?" I asked.

"I don't give two Yankee shits where they go as long as it's not in front of our shop," said Ben. "They can go back wherever they came from."

"They have no place to go."

"That's not my fault."

"But it is!" flew out of my mouth. I'm not sure I believed this first parry, but with each subsequent thrust, my conviction gained strength.

"How is it our fault?" Ben's voice had jumped far beyond its regular loud.

"Roger," warned Trip.

"Don't shush me, Trip! We're all responsible."

"We are? Who is *we*?" said Trip.

"This country is rigged against the poor!" Now *I* was shouting.

Late capitalism and its depredations were unfamiliar terrain in my early twenties, but I did know that Reagan and Congress had passed legislation that pushed mentally ill people onto the streets of New Haven. Crack addiction and poverty and crime and vagrancy were interrelated issues. The Sterling cataloguers at least had Local 34 to protect them. I told the table that no one was looking out for homeless people, and that it was wrong to just sweep them out of sight.

"The poor have their own bootstraps to pull themselves up with," said Till, using that ghastly commonplace.

"That's bullshit, Till!" I shouted. "Look at where we are right now!"

We panned the bouquets of parrot tulips on the Biedermeier surfaces in the dining room, and the king's ransom of silver, crystal, and porcelain beneath our hands. On the walls were old Tilghman portraits, and an 18th century map of their many estates on the Eastern Shore of Maryland. Till had once told me, not without pride, that the Revolutionary War had divided the family.

Matthew 26:11: "The poor you will always have with you."

What I should have said is that poverty is not a crime, shut my trap, and let them stew in that truth. But I didn't come from wealth, and my gender meant that Trip and I would be unable to pass on our capital to Quartz and Quintus Hauf-Buttenwieser. With a final flare of self-righteousness, I pointed to the map over the buffet and asked how many people the Tilghman family had enslaved back in the day.

There was no point in staying. The farewells were glacial.

In high school, I had taken a course called "Family Living." In the unit on marital compatibility, Mr. Zarcone neglected to teach us that mutual respect is one relationship *sine qua non* that helps a couple through the tough times. No surprise, really, at Zarcone's curricular lapse—I mean, at sixteen, who knows, much less values, what respect is? On the ride home, I told Trip that his wish to still be straight had diminished my respect for him, and that I didn't know where that left us.

"Ha!" he said, eyes on the road. "That makes two of us, Roger."

"What do you mean? I may be from nothing, but that's no reason not to respect me."

"Yes, you made that point clear when you called Till a slavemaster."

"I'll apologize for my manners; don't you worry about that."

We drove on. Squirming at the end of his hook, I finally asked him why he didn't respect me.

"Elayne Colton forced me out of the closet. What's your story?"

"What?"

"You're still a closet case, Roger."

"I'm out."

"Not your parents in Nebraska. Not to any of your relatives."

"They know I'm gay. Please."

"Not from your own lips they don't."

Trip had held this trump, but had chosen not to play it, or let it affect his feelings for me. And what role had he played in my sudden championing of the poor? His plan for our future, after all, was engineered to keep me off the mean streets of Manhattan. In his eyes, was I that helpless? Or hapless?

Things weren't the same after that Bucks County weekend when I learned that I had some politics. You can't expect a misalliance set in motion by two sex dreams and a pinkie ring to *improve,* can you? Dreams like that are a warning, not an invitation.

We still had the summer of '86 to get through. Trip spent his weeks in New York interning for the Nederlanders but came home on weekends. By June, I found I could no longer kiss him without blowing air into his cheeks as a joke. He cheated on me in New York. I cheated on him in New Haven. I don't know who cheated first. I wrote mean letters about him to David Towle in Naples. He took a hammer to his onyx brooch and left its carcass on my desk. I scorched fifty *Roger Hale Hauf* notecards over the gas stove, then left the envelopes in the box on my old bed.

Trip never became a Broadway producer. After a couple of decades in personal portfolio management, he and his life partner (now husband and adoptive co-father of two) left Manhattan and the private sector and moved to Baltimore. He began raising money for an academy dedicated to sending its entire student body of Black women to college. Seven years ago, the school was the subject of an Oscar-nominated documentary; when I read the credit, "*Associate Producer* Ross Gerald Buttenweiser III," I saw that, true to his people, he did right by the common weal, whereas I teach dramatic literature to the turbocharged progeny of the 1%, and the occasional scholarship student at a highly selective Quaker college.

Today, the percentage of urban mendicants fluctuates according to policy changes and how well or poorly the markets behave. However, as aggregates of socioeconomic co-morbidities set in motion—cynics would say "set in stone"—by the monied class as far back as Colonial Maryland, unhoused Americans are never going to disappear.

At one time, I looked forward to becoming a gay uncle like Benjamin Sachsen and Gough Thompson Tilghman, wise and entertaining and solicitous, keen to pass on knowledge and traditions, and pick up the check. The global reach of the Internet and its embrace of queers and all of their cross-pollinating cultures, however, have rendered the position of homosexual lifestyle mentor as quaint and as obsolete as a tomato lift.

Nightstand

"How soon can you be out of here?" asked Louis, my husband of eighteen months.

I had come home to Philadelphia from a conference in Milwaukee and remarked, as we were prepping for bed, that I felt as if it didn't seem to matter to him which city I was in. That set off a monologue that began with the statement that he was feeling "hopeless about the marriage."

The third floor was frigid that January night. From a metal folding chair, its seat covered with dried paint drips, I listened to Louis say crushing things about me. He was a psychiatrist, an initial blessing that had become, over time, an unfair advantage because it led me to receive every negative from his direction as gospel truth. If it had been his shrink's strategy to incite me to push back against his rulings, it failed every time. I believed him no matter what.

I leaned against the flank of a Stickley armoire I had bought for us in less hopeless times. The unstained floor was scribbled with grooves too deep to be sanded smooth. It looked as if a child had mounted a circular saw and had been riding it like a tricycle. Replacing the wood was far down on Louis's list of home projects. He'd grown up on a sugar beet farm in North Dakota. His ability to wire, plumb, lay sheetrock and tile, build a brick wall, hang wallpaper, garden, cook, and can fruits and vegetables, had drawn me to him. He'd dug a goldfish pond, built a grape trellis in the backyard, installed a shower. I'd been his helper, grunt, and *assistant de chef*. With guests, I was as house-proud as he was.

As Louis spoke, I focused on his black-painted nightstand behind him and to the left, its open mouth packed tight with old bills, concert programs, patient notes, and, occasionally, a pornographic magazine, which was a big issue for me. When we were dating, I'd had this notion that with me beside him Louis wouldn't need porn. How could I not be enough? I hated having to look for his porn as much as I hated finding it. When feeling particularly insecure, I'd search with the fury of Carrie Nation until I'd found a stash under his car seat, or in the magazine basket in our bathroom, or under a pile of grocery bags in the pantry. We had stopped discussing how I felt they demeaned me, so I'd stack them on his side of the bed and wait for them to disappear.

As I listened, I didn't interrupt Louis to advocate for our union when he had decided, unilaterally, that he was dissolving it. The Supreme Court wouldn't grant the right to same-sex marriage for decades, so we had wed ourselves to one another in the spring of 1995, in a ceremony of our own devising, in front of eighty-seven guests in the garden of a friend's house in Society Hill. At the time my T-cell count was thirty-five. Statistics forecast two more years before my inevitable death from AIDS. Yet when I had said, "I do" to Louis, I was not ill, or weak, or depressed, or anxious about anything beyond whether the food would hold out, and our guests would dance to the swing band we had hired for the reception.

One afternoon, late in 1996, after five months on the brand-new antiretroviral combination therapy, I learned that my HIV viral load was undetectable and that my T-cells were climbing. I drove Louis's car back from the doctor's office and devoured a Greek salad while parked in the driveway. When the magnitude of the news finally sunk in, I stained my tie and trousers with a falling ring of green pepper. If I was going to live— and Dr. Butson had suggested that this was definitely the case—then I decided that I needed to work on my marriage.

I kept this decision from Louis, but it was on my mind when, the week after Christmas, I found a trove of pornographic tapes in the Stickley cabinet in his first-floor office where he saw private patients. *Bad Black Daddies* is the title that sticks most in my mind, because the red ball jammed in the hog-tied submissive's mouth on the box looked particularly obscene. Presenting the evidence, I said to him, "Magazines are horrible enough, but *movies* too? We don't own a television, Louis. Where do you watch these?"

"There's a VHS deck in my group practice office."

"Do you watch them during office hours? Between patients? Or before you come home to me?"

"I watch mostly on weekends." His voice remained perfectly even.

"*Mostly?*"

Behind him, lending clinical support on a shelf in a glass cabinet, stood my extravagant Christmas Gift of 1996: the twenty-four volumes of Freud's *Standard Edition,* in pale blue dust wrappers.

I shoved the cassette box in his face. "*Bad Black Daddies*? I'm not any one of those three things."

"I know," he replied, relieving me of my sad little weapon.

Now, a month later, frozen in the folding chair against the armoire, I had no choice but to accept his final judgment. He said he had never been happy with me. He said he had to work too fucking hard to get so little air. He said I didn't recognize him as a complete and separate person. He said I completely invalidated him. I believe he had gone on in that vein for twenty minutes before I managed to interrupt him, in a tiny voice: "What would have happened if I had gotten sick?"

He said, "I would have stayed with you, Roger."

In sickness, but not in health. Then I said, in an even tinier voice, practically a squeak, "Lucky for you, I got better, huh?"

"The person I am becoming can't be with the person you are."

And that's when he had asked how soon I could be out of his house.

I plucked my eyeglasses from the window embrasure and a pillow from my side of our Mission-style sleigh bed, then crossed the hallway to the guest room. I hadn't disagreed whenever Louis called me a righteous control freak, but stealing the very air from him? That was tantamount to murder. Silly me to think that exchanging vows in front of eighty-seven people meant that when a couple hits a wall, they would at least *attempt* to unbrick it together. Stay together, fly apart, but *try*. Louis's work was based on the conviction that people could change, but he had denied that possibility in me, and for us.

When I came downstairs the next morning, the pocket door to the back parlor was closed, which meant Louis was with a patient. I quietly set my weekender against the bottom step. We had spent weeks stripping and sanding all three flights of the staircase to his specifications but had yet to start painting them. There were one hundred and seventy-four spokes waiting for the brush. Also, an unfinished dining room on the second floor whose balcony door opened onto a thirty-foot drop into the fishpond. The third-floor toilet still wasn't hooked up. The only project he finished was me.

For my final act as household help, I went to the magazine stand in the front parlor, where his patients waited to see him, and placed well-thumbed copies of *Honcho*, *Inches*, *Bound & Gagged*, and *Freshman* magazines under the latest issues of *Town & Country*, *Harper's*, and *National Geographic*. Louis's patients, I thought, should have a clearer picture of who was treating them. I went outside and flagged a cab. The police siren that went off a couple of blocks away just then sounded like church bells.

Worth Our Breath

I opened the 'B' section of the *Inquirer* and read that Brian Whipke, securities lawyer, was dead from stomach cancer, aged fifty-three. There was no photo. I debated calling E.F., who clearly had left for the hospital without getting to the paper. He would have woken me up with the news otherwise. Besides shock, I wasn't sure what I felt.

Neither of us had seen or even run into Brian in at least a decade. The obit didn't mention a surviving partner. I wondered whether Tom Schwarz had known of Brian's illness and whether he would come down from New York to attend the viewing in Bala Cynwyd. I wondered whether we would. Or, to be honest, whether I would. E.F., always able to forgive, would certainly go. I sat with the paper until my coffee got cold, remembering how we had been friends with Brian and Tom and why and how our friendship had ended. The decision had been mine.

It begins and ends with children. Mere weeks into our relationship, E.F. had offered to adopt a child with me; gays and lesbians were doing so in increasing numbers at the time, but we both knew that Olive, our dumpster rescue kitten with the shot gums and wary disdain of a meth addict, was all I could manage. I loved Olive to pieces, and she gave *nothing* back. She'd approach for tuna water and dairy, and that was it. If, for example, she had begun peeing outside the litter box, she'd have been back on Germantown Avenue in ten minutes. That's the kind of father I'd make.

In 2006, when Tom Schwarz first met Brian Whipkey, E.F. and I had been together for five years. He was and is a research nurse at Jefferson Hospital, and I've taught dramatic literature at Haverford since the dawn of time. We were then in our mid-forties, and compared to the other male couples we knew in our age bracket, E.F. and I had no assets besides his family silver and a couple of portraits. We lived in a converted condo in Mt. Airy, an easy walk to the colonial showplaces of our rich friends in Chestnut Hill. I liked to think we couldn't be bought.

We did have something no one else had, something dearer than Brunschwig & Fils wallpaper or a weekend place in Delaware: E.F.'s four fully grown, biological children, three girls and a boy he had delivered himself in a tepee on a Santa Cruz commune in the seventies. Their mother had left after weaning Rory, and E.F. raised them himself, canning fish and picking Brussels sprouts to keep them fed. He doesn't think so, but his is quite the story.

Five years and we had never had a fight. A month into dating E.F., I knew I'd start inventing conflicts unless I returned for a little preventive therapy. Dr. Thorne endured my rants about this sexed-up nurturer who had to be a sociopath *somehow* until I realized that getting his ducklings through each and every day for twenty-five years had bleached E.F. free of aggression, ego strivings, and a siege mentality—all of my burdens. Before we terminated treatment, Thorne did say that I shouldn't be surprised if our first fight would be over E.F. having to choose between a child and me. I couldn't picture that happening, since three of them lived on the West Coast, and the eldest, gorgeous Celestia over in Elwyn, was too much like me in the righteousness department to sow dissent amongst the elders.

Every year during the last week of June, E.F. and dozens of Fowlers, great and small, vacation in the Outer Banks in Duck, North Carolina. The summer of Brian and Tom, there were almost thirty of us spread across four houses on Pintail Drive. I'd learned from previous Duck weeks that the Fowlers were so loving and generous with one another that even if I joined in their reindeer games, or maybe because I had, by Wednesday, I'd be depressed for my own family. Put it this way: our rental slept nine, yet, like as not, in the morning, I'd find three or four Fowler cousins cuddled on the living room couches like a litter of puppies. My brother Bud and I had grown up like scorpions in a jar.

Because my cheap Irish skin prevented any semblance of a tan, I'd spend prime beach hours gossiping indoors with whichever sister-in-law was slated to feed the hordes that night. I was slicing farm stand tomatoes when I heard a car pull up. It could have been a subset of Fowlers coming back from putt-putt or the T-shirt emporia, but then I heard a distinctive booming laugh over the door slams.

I went to one of the six wooden decks that every cockamamie beach rental in Duck seems to have. Brian Whipke and Tom Schwarz were climbing out of a red convertible jeep.

"What are you doing here?" I called out.

"Heading to Ocracoke," said Tom. "Surprised?"

"Absolutely," I said, meaning it. E.F. must have given them our address.

"Can you put us up for the night, Roger?" asked Brian, emptying the dregs of a Mountain Dew on the driveway. Brian Whipke never looked at you directly when he asked for something.

"Absolutely."

Tom stretched his arms above his head as he came around the back of the jeep and then circled Brian's waist from behind. I expected a flinch, or the kind of struggle Olive put up when I ambushed her, but Brian rubbed his head against Tom's ear as he shook the tension out of his legs. Progress in the PDA department, I thought, a moment to share later with E.F.

Brian was an old friend of E.F.'s who brought box mix brownies to our house most Mondays for dinner. In a pinch, he'd drive us to the airport, but still, I thought he could put himself out more. Two eggs and a cup of water, I'd grumble to E.F., usually after Brian had spent another dinner ducking my questions. I'd never been inside his apartment, a fortress near Drexel that he rented to be closer to Wilmington for his daily commute. He had, by every account, an extremely large penis. This last fact, repeated like scripture over the bridge tables and bar carts of lavender Chestnut Hill, irked me. It wasn't vulgar *per se*, or uninteresting, but it bothered me nonetheless that I should have to keep hearing about it. We may lead with our junk when young, but our set of friends had mortgages and sciatica flare-ups. If having a horse dick revealed, or justified, more of Brian's lone wolf persona, it might be worth our breath, but why, in our forties, should it remain an ace of trumps?

Tom Schwarz was a Beckett specialist from New York City whom I'd brought to Haverford for a modern drama symposium that January. Before law school, Brian Whipke had tried to be a set designer, so he and

Tom had a common subject when I introduced them at the boozy opening reception for the visiting scholars. The novelty for E.F. and me was seeing Brian's hand on Tom's shoulder, and the way his pelvis tilted in. Brian was putting himself literally forward, and Tom, unhappily single, with silver hair and hangdog looks, seemed to lose ten years with the attention. Some Mondays later, we knew to ask no questions of Brian upon learning that Tom was coming down to see cousins "in Lancaster," but I know that we were proud at having set a pair of men up; it was proof that our love was communicable. And now, they'd taken another cue and followed our trail to the Outer Banks.

I invited them up for a gin-and-tonic, but they had made a pact to run straight for the ocean. Standing in the gulley between their jeep and E.F.'s leaky old Honda, they shucked their shirts and shoes and tossed them into a common pile in the back seat. Another sign of a meld.

"You're going to get burnt," I called after them.

I went to our house to get my sun hat. Mercy and Rebecca, E.F.'s second and third daughters, were in the kitchen, clawing boulders of macaroni and cheese out of a giant foil pan. We'd hosted the feed the night before, the young people falling over my apple crisp, or at least pretending to. My not-so-secret ingredient is grated raw ginger. I told the girls that Brian Whipke had shown up—with *a boyfriend*—and they squealed and ran out with beers for them. I pushed away a flutter of jealousy, reminding myself that they had known Brian longer than me. E.F. the kids, and Brian had bicycled Nantucket on the cheap one summer, camping or staying in hostels, and doing charcoal rubbings of ancient Fowler gravestones. As far as I'm concerned, camping is the final circle of hell, right after live jazz, but part of me sometimes wished I were outdoorsy and spontaneous.

✳

The wind whiffling my hair was fresh and cool. I counted fourteen towels, six beach chairs, and three umbrellas. When E.F., brown as butterscotch sauce, waved from the water, I teared up. In moments like these, I was grateful to be even a weed in the Fowler cabbage patch. Time and again, I resisted cynical claims from the garden queens of Chestnut Hill that all male couples will eventually cheat, or craft extramarital arrangements. I knew I would never be mature enough or bored enough or stupid enough to share my E.F. In meeting him, I had lain down my arms, and he had washed me clean. (As an objective correlative, my viral load had been undetectable for nearly ten years, and my T-cell count remained in the 500-600 range.)

Celestia marked her place in her book with a finger. "So that's Tom," she whispered to me. She often rode in with Brian and his brownies on Monday nights. "Interesting."

"How so?" I asked.

"The silver hair."

"He's only forty-nine." E.F. and I weren't that far behind him.

"I would have thought he'd be hotter."

This last surprised me. I asked whether she thought Brian was hot. He was out on a sandbar with E.F., too far off for me to gauge his legendary equipment in wet board shorts. Celestia shrugged in a way that meant she did, and I felt another flutter of jealousy. That the kids might have hoped for their father to pair up with Brian had never occurred to me. Our coming together had been so instant and so joyous I simply assumed that E.F. had been waiting all his life for me. Our song—his pick—is Etta James's "At Last."

Tom motioned me over. He had a big grin on his face. "This came Wednesday," he said. He tucked his beer bottle under an arm, fished a money clip out of a side pocket in his cargo pants, and then set something gently onto my palm.

It was a passport-sized photo of an Asian child.

"Who is that?"

"My daughter. Elise. I'm adopting her from China."

It's a tricky moment. The New Testament doesn't mention a friend of Mary or Elizabeth who wondered about the wisdom of their pregnancies. No one had urged sterilization on my father, and with ten (!) of their own, E.F.'s parents hadn't questioned his having four on a Brussels sprout picker's wages. So, when you don't know the adoptive gay dad all that well, you congratulate him and ask easy logistical questions— How soon? How long is the plane ride? How long will you be over there?

Where will she get her shots?—rather than, can you afford her *really*, where will the crib in a one-bedroom walk-up in Spanish Harlem go, and have you done the math on how old you'll be when she starts high school?

Elise's hair, and there was a lot of it, was parted on the left with a barrette. Her face was full, almost pudgy, and I interpreted her sober expression as a request to please take her to America. She wasn't smiling, nor, I decided, should she have been. If she were smiling, how would she learn to be grateful?

E.F. sprinted up the beach. I made him dry his hands, then passed him the photo and poured on the enthusiasm. "Tom is going to be a father. He's flying next month to Jiangxi to get Elise."

"On August 18th," Tom clarified.

E.F. studied the photo, ran a fingertip along its edges as if he were measuring the dimensions of Elise's cell at the orphanage. He adored babies and had been a neonatal nurse before starting his research job, so his silence felt off to me.

"Did you get your plane ticket?" I asked Tom.

"And a new passport. After three years I can't believe it's finally going to happen. China is getting stricter about single fathers adopting girls."

E.F. handed the picture back to Tom. "That's a long time to wait. Is this your first look at her?"

"It is," said Tom, tilting the photo this way and that to catch more light or information. "She's older than the agency said she'd be. I thought I was getting a baby, but she's actually twenty months."

"Twenty months," said E.F.

A drifting cloud threw a shadow, or something passed between them. At any rate, I felt the temperature drop. "That's almost two," I said, trying to be helpful.

"You don't think that's a problem, do you?" asked Tom.

"Heavens no," said E.F. "She's a beautiful toddler, and I think what you're doing is wonderful, Tom."

I looked around for beautiful, corroborating toddlers. There was a darling pair just at the edge of the ocean, jerking pails with their slightly spastic arms as they outran their mothers.

Tom shaded his eyes in the direction of a booming offshore laugh. E.F. and I shared a look. Tom Schwarz might fly to China in mid-August to pick up his daughter, Elise, but this I knew: When Brian Whipke brought us box mix brownies, he set the dish at the far end of our dining room table and sped away from them, arms folded.

✳

That night, Brian and Tom camped out in our living room, zipping their sleeping bags together like teenagers. They'd also fixed plates for one other, and I'd caught a kiss on a porch. I joked later, as E.F. and I went to bed, that Brian was in danger of domestication.

E.F. flipped up his side of the covers. In another forty years, he'd have the same arch to his back as his father. I looked forward to being there to see it. Sliding a leg under the sheet, he said, out of the blue, not like him at all, "They send the pictures to help the bonding process, but it's not working."

"What are you talking about?"

"Tom is having second thoughts."

I sat up. "What makes you say that?"

"I've watched him look at the picture. On the beach, and all during dinner."

"And?"

"She doesn't look the way he wants her to."

"How should she look?"

"Like a brilliant waif eager to come to America and learn the violin."

"You're nuts," I said. "We toasted Elise non-stop. He took us through the whole megillah. He can't back out at the last minute."

E.F. set his watch on the nightstand. "The thing is, honey, at twenty months, who the child is, and who she is going to be, is formed. She's already marked."

I thought of the signs saying "Final Clearance" at the Nordstrom's Rack in Center City, where I shopped for sheets and towels. They carried luxury menswear too, but the shoes and jackets were in impossible colors, like butterscotch or mint, or impossible sizes. When merchandise is discounted repeatedly, something's wrong with it.

"But once you've picked the baby, don't you have to take it?" I asked.

"Tom didn't pick her; the orphanage did."

I drew up my legs. On our second date, E.F. had told me how it had felt to deliver his own children. He'd gotten the first look as they slid into his hands. Rebecca took the longest, Celestia was the loudest, Mercy came out smiling, and Rory, after three girls, was the surprise package. E.F. had cut their cords, buried their placentas, and because he had only a motorcycle for transport, he had carried them in his arms down a mountain to register them with the state of California. He'd done their Apgar scores at one and five minutes. All were perfectly red, squalling, taut-toned creatures waiting to be loved.

"If she were crippled, or mentally delayed or something, they would have told him, wouldn't they?"

E.F. opened his eyes. "Not necessarily. The Russians don't. The Romanians don't."

I pulled one of his hands out of the covers and bounced it on my knee. "Tom *wants* Elise."

"Tom wants his idea of Elise. A Suzuki-trained neurobiologist."

"That's a horrible thing to say."

"He has a need, and an image, and they don't match up."

"That's just a crazy hunch you have," I said, aware that E.F. never had crazy hunches. Rather than agree with him, I turned away and pitched the softer of my pillows to the floor. It felt like the start of a first fight until he began scratching the small of my back.

"I hope I'm wrong, honey, but I've watched thousands of mothers and fathers with their babies."

I had a new thought. "What about Daddy Number Two? The withholder." At dinner, Brian had raised his glass to Elise like everybody else and chimed in at key points during Tom's adoption saga, but as ever, he resisted interpretation.

"Hmmm," said E.F., neither spurring me on nor shutting me off. "That will be interesting."

I dragged my foot up the side of his leg. "Have you seen Brian's penis?

"I don't think so."

"'You don't *think* so'? If it's the tonsil-tearing monster everyone says it is, you'd remember."

"Take my head off," he said mildly.

(This was code for "Why are you getting worked up, Roger?")

I pressed again. "How about on Nantucket that summer? In the men's shower room?"

He gave me a look. He was tired and done with the subject. There was no reason not to believe him.

E.F. goes out cold in four minutes—the sleep of the just—but my brain doesn't shut off easily. Except for the hum of the refrigerator, the house was quiet; the young people were on the beach with a bonfire and chests of beer. An abrupt yowl outside reminded me that our adoptee, Olive, had to be thrilled to be left alone for a week with only a neighbor to open cans for her. Our vet, Dr. Geis, had been recommending a full dental extraction. It would stop her bleeding gums and halt the inflammation that often led to kidney failure, but spending seventeen hundred dollars on a cat, especially one whose sole objective in life was to avoid us, seemed absurd.

Without even leaving Jiangxi, Elise had already cost Tom close to twelve thousand dollars. I watched the sheet rise and fall with E.F.s breathing and began to focus on the little girl. I admit that I began to appraise her potential through the lens of the cynical, childless materialists we played bridge and brunched with in Philadelphia. This cost-benefit analysis, if you will, led me to conclude that Elise Schwarz wasn't a waif. She wasn't a genius. She was a peasant, one of six billion, or whatever the Chinese population currently stood at. It would be too late for her to start the violin. She would grow up to become the kind of New Yorker who sat across from you in a subway car, slack and tired, feet turned in, hair loosely gathered, on her way home from a service job scooping fries with a stainless steel shovel, or sliding noodles into vats of boiling water.

✳

E. F.'s hunch was right. Two weeks later Tom, via a group e-mail, said he was halting the adoption. He ducked all opportunities to elaborate, so there would never be a more specific reason than his having, and I quote, "underestimated the all-consuming time commitment it took to raise a child," unquote. I can't imagine what his old friends, who had presumably supported him through the entire quest felt, but I was furious. What else would a child *be* but eighteen years of time and attention? E.F. hadn't thrown in the towel when his ex-wife took off and left him with four kids under the age of five

When the subject came up—and it was hard for me to drop—E.F. stuck to his theory that something in Elise's face had changed Tom's mind. My theory began and ended with Brian Whipke. If you're pushing fifty, and you've been alone for years, and you want a life partner, you are not going to sacrifice the possibility of romantic love, even from a lone wolf, for a semi-abstract toddler ten time zones away.

By Christmas that year, Tom was splitting his weeks between New York and Philadelphia. He rented a waterfront duplex in Penn's Landing while Brian stuck to his University City fortress. Tom always brought wine and a side dish to our Monday dinners, and reciprocated with thoughtful meals of his own. He often thanked us for setting them up, but Brian still could not be made to refer to Tom as his boyfriend. The looks he'd shoot when I asked when they'd sign a lease together were priceless.

They were outdoorsy. They visited Gettysburg and Antietam and Valley Forge, camped and kayaked at the Delaware Water Gap, hiked in Glen Onoko Falls, and rode mountain bikes to Harrisburg. They'd return from their expeditions with finds for Tom's rental: iron wall brackets, a church pew, tramp art candlesticks. They re-purposed a privy door and a sheet of crackle glass into a dining room table, and a curd press into a nightstand. They set up Tom's model trains on a piece of plywood and painted a *trompe l'oeil* village around the tracks.

I had begun to resent their self-sufficiency until E.F. reminded me that we had had our own year of nesting, and moreover, I'd rather die than get into a kayak. Some part of me must have wanted Tom and Brian to treat us as their sponsors to the bougie pursuits of Chestnut Hill, because I was flattered when they asked us to teach them how to play bridge. After a few lessons, they joined the two tables that rotated among four houses. Tom studied the book we'd loaned him, but Brian played erratically. Some of the regulars fought to be his partner and seemed to excuse his reckless bidding on the grounds that men with horse dicks could devise their own point count systems.

Then, one April day, we got a message from Brian saying that bridge was out that week because he and Tom had split up—on Brian's initiative. Tom said later, in near hysterics, that Brian had offered no reasons and worst of all, hadn't had the decency to tell him *in person*. In a rare, judgmental moment, E.F. said that Brian's breaking up over the phone demeaned all gay men.

It rained the entire Saturday that we packed Tom up. When we walked into his apartment, soaked from a dash across the parking lot, there was a sheaf of unmade boxes standing against the sofa. I made a face. If you are relying on friends for labor, not being packed is an unpardonable offense.

Tom, wrapping dishes in the dining room, smelled sour, and his eyes were red. I went into the kitchen and found Brian eating a doughnut. Powdered sugar crusted the mouth of the juice carton in his other hand. My glacial hello was returned with a lift of his brows. As soon as E.F. and I got into the hallway with the first load, I kicked a box and hissed that Tom should have had the self-respect to keep Brian away.

The duplex was in a converted sailcloth factory; to reach the loading dock, we had to navigate Tom's stuff down long halls into a tiny elevator that kept stopping for yuppies in workout gear. Tom hadn't thought to buy rope, and two of the three small dollies he had secured from the super had wandering wheels, which slowed us down. Because the relationship was beyond treatment, Tom seemed to be using the transfer of his objects as a therapy session. E.F. and I would return from the dock to find them discussing whether the sofa should come before or after the desk, and what about the giant clown poster? More than once Tom called us back from the door to say, "Wait—that can't go in yet. I have to think about it." The mattress was the final thing we hauled out. The ghostly patterns of semen stains on its quilted top looked like a Qing Dynasty painting of anemones.

It took nine hours. By the time we reached U-Store-It, the rain, and the humidity, and our exhaustion made the boxes slide from our arms, but the dollies there were solid and sturdy. E.F. and I fled as soon as Tom's effects were heaped around the entrance to his chicken-wire storage coop. Pizza and beer with them would have been horrible, and we had to clean up for the symphony. As we trudged down a cement alley toward the elevator, we could hear them discuss the best placement for the lamps, as if the cage weren't a mausoleum for Tom's hopes, but that modest starter apartment they had been planning to rent all along.

Celestia came by herself to dinner the following Monday. She liked our new slipcovers, which we had waited to have done until after Olive's gums healed from the dental extraction. Dr. Geis had given us Olive's teeth—some of their shapes were hugely strange—in a plastic, snap-top tooth that, when you shook it, sounded like a seventeen-hundred-dollar baby rattle. Geis said she would be free of mouth pain for the first time in her life, and although her disposition had yet to improve, there were no more blood spots on the upholstery.

While E.F. whipped cream in the kitchen, I took Celestia through the ghastly moving day. My arms and back were still sore from all the lifting.

"If Tom is storing his things in Philly," she said, "he must think he can get Brian back."

E.F. brought in coffee and dessert. "He still loves him. Tom said these had been the happiest fifteen months of his life, so he's keeping the door open."

"The back door," I scoffed, purposely vulgar. "Tom was too needy. You could see it coming when Brian rented that absurdly priced duplex."

E.F. laughed. He often said, usually referring to me, that people love to have seen things coming. I topped Celestia's slice of berry tart with whipped cream and said, "Desperation isn't a good look on anyone."

"He kept hoping," said E.F. "When we played tennis last month, he was busting to tell me that Brian was asleep in his apartment. Having Brian stay the night for the first time was a breakthrough."

"You never told me that," I said. I lowered a teaspoon of cream for Olive. She'd come for it, as long as I didn't watch her.

"It would only have pissed you off," said E.F.

It did piss me off. That E.F. knew it would piss me off pissed me off even more. I felt the spoon handle bob from the pressure of Olive's tongue and pictured Brian Whipke snoring on Tom's mattress, his dirty underwear on the floor, a thermos of coffee and a fresh frittata in a Pyrex dish on the kitchen counter downstairs, a note underneath on how long to keep it in the oven, and at what temperature, and when Tom would be back xoxoxo.

"It must really be that big," I said.

"What's that big?" said Celestia.

"Honey," warned E.F.

I shrugged. Celestia, twenty-seven, knew her way around a penis. "Men with big dicks always get off scot-free," I said, trying (and failing) to be funny about this flaw in our subculture. "But this time a child was involved."

"A child?" said Celestia. "What child?"

Clearly, she didn't remember that giddy supper at Duck, or the toasts made to a photograph propped against a bowl filled with ceramic starfish, but I did. I'd stopped saying her name in my head, but I had not forgotten Elise. The promise of her was hidden in a North Philly storage space, a pudgy face packed into a box of mixing bowls or slipped into the drawer of a curd press nightstand, or waiting in the seat of a model train car for someone to trip the switch and take her to America. I had never been able to shake the feeling that because we'd introduced Brian to Tom, E.F. and I had helped put her there.

"That's between them, Roger," said E.F. "It's their business."

"Tom picked that careless prick over that child. And now he has neither. It serves him right."

"You would have done the same thing."

"You're absolutely right!" I exploded. I could tell E.F. had sat on his observation for months, but in my own way, I had been waiting for him to say it. "I would certainly have chosen you over a child, E.F. But on the other hand, I wouldn't have, because I wouldn't have been so stupid as to think I had any business raising a child to begin with."

"People can change their minds."

"No! Not in this case. Children are not commodities. Elise was worth saving. It was a crime to let her go."

"It is better for that girl—"

"Elise!"

"That was *Tom's* name for her. It's better that she stayed in China. She couldn't have known someone was coming for her."

"And no one ever will!"

"An unfortunate thing happened, but it wasn't a crime."

"It was worse than a crime—it was a *whim*!"

"Get off your high horse, Roger."

"Get off my *what*?"

Olive raced from the room at the change in my voice.

"Stop being so self-righteous. You were as needy as Tom was when I first met you."

"What? I was *never* that needy—"

"I was too, I suppose."

"You weren't, E.F.," I said. "And don't try to placate me by saying you were. I hate it when you do that."

"Fine," he snapped, in a tone that he had never taken with me. Celestia actually gasped to hear it. "I won't."

"You weren't needy."

"Need is not a crime, Roger."

"It is. It most certainly is—"

I stopped.

So, there it was, our first fight, or at least its beginning, since even in the moment E.F. made his point, I suspected it might take me the rest of my born days to agree with him. I had somehow managed to get away with my life of crime. My needs had been met, finally, miraculously. I would still have to face the greater challenge of accepting my win at the game of life while Elise was denied the chance even to enter the casino.

At some point in the next year I had a strained lunch in Manhattan with Tom Schwarz. We still track each other down at academic conferences. E.F. and I never invited the late Brian Whipke to our home again. According to the *Inquirer*, there would be a mass of Christian burial at Holy Trinity Lutheran in Narberth on Wednesday morning, followed by a private interment.

All these years later, I can't say that I would call things any differently. Need and its many appointments were, and are, for me, as they say today, a trigger. At the time, I recall picking up my fork, aware that Celestia was watching me, aware that Olive, safe on the porch, was combing an ear. Dr. Thorne had been partially correct. A child had come between us, but not one of E.F.'s. Then E.F., protecting us all, brought up our impending trip to Corsica, and I cut into my piece of the tart.

Service Learning

Lt. Hailey, a jarhead who had clearly aced the Presidential Fitness Test every year in grade school, had no visible reaction to my assertion that all women of quality have had at least one gay boyfriend in their pasts.

I wasn't being facetious, but I did wonder whether, with his crewcut and boxy brown suit, the thirtysomething Lt. Hailey was as resistant to humor as I assumed all government personnel were. He had barged into my office one late afternoon just as I'd packed to leave, posing three questions in a tone that required immediate answers. Had I ever been intimately involved with a woman named Audrey Carrigan? "Yes." Was I primarily homosexual? "Certainly." Did I know what chlordecone was? "No."

A surprise visitor with a military title from Arlington, VA—and we know what that means, or think we do—asking me about someone whom I hadn't heard of or from in decades made me anxious. Yet I was also contemptuous enough a blue stater in these grim times to resent federal intrusion. Choosing not to yield further ground, I locked eyes with Henrik Ibsen on the wall poster behind his left shoulder (Ibsen lends strength in a challenge) and made the quip about all women of quality having had one gay boyfriend. Then I asked the Lieutenant, whose ring finger was bare, whether there was a Mrs. Hailey.

"Maybe," he answered. He pulled the door closed behind him.

"You're not sure?" I parried, an emcee with a balky guest.

"Whether there is or isn't a Mrs. Hailey isn't your business, Dr. Hauf. Tell me about Audrey Carrigan."

"You may think we're in a police procedural, Lieutenant Hailey, but you haven't provided the kind of identification I would need to answer your rude request."

I re-zipped my laptop case and was reaching to click off my desk lamp when he said, "There is a Ms. Hailey. But how is she germane to the discussion?"

[Point scored for "germane."]

"Do you consider your wife to be a woman of quality?"

"Ms. Hailey is my mother."

"Do you consider your mother to be a woman of quality?"

His smile was disarming. "My mother was, and remains, a bubble-headed tomato, Roger."

So there was a sense of humor in there, and I could tell the boy still loved his mother. For a split-second, I thought he might be the one gay man in a million who wore tan leather shoes. Then I thought he was going to tell me he was my son with Audrey Carrigan, a standard reveal in classical theater.

"Get your mother to tell you one day about the boyfriend she had who turned out to be gay."

"Her generation doesn't talk about things like that," said Lt. Hailey, sounding like he thought the present generation talked it to death. I wouldn't disagree with him there.

We listened to the bell tower chime five o'clock. I decided against offering him a drink. I'd be pegged as another academic souse with bourbon in the desk drawer. Dead, alive, doing time, or on the lam, what had Audrey Carrigan been up to that would cause a G-man to visit a past-it drama professor in outer Philadelphia?

I closed my eyes to remember my first glimpse of Audrey Carrigan. It was June 1984, in Sénégal, West Africa. I had just disembarked from a fishing boat that had taken me up the coast from the capital port, Dakar, to a village called Mboro Ndeundekat. I'd dropped my duffel to stretch my jetlagged self when a white woman addressed me in French. I traveled up her voluminous linen skirt in a harlequinade pattern of blue, white, red, and yellow patches. One hand held a netted bag of mangoes. Her free wrist was bent over her forehead to keep the sun at bay.

My initial thought was, "Boy, do I want to try on that skirt." On her approach, one of her heels wobbled in the macadam, which caused her to fall onto me. Her apology sounded charmingly insincere, quite as if she often pitched into strangers as a way to disarm them...

Lt. Hailey was on his phone now, another impertinence. "It's a simple question," I heard him say, his back to me. "I *said,* cast your mind back." Audrey and the landing dock disappeared.

A lifetime in team sports had given him permission to annex my space. He tipped spines on my bookshelves, rubbed the dust on the leaves of the succulent on the windowsill, gnawed idly at a fingernail. He'd spit the paring onto the carpet, I knew, if I wasn't watching. He finished his call with, "Okay then, Saturday," and slipped his phone into a breast pocket. He turned, and with another smile, said, "You win, Roger."

"I do?"

"My mother thinks Charlie Sizer was a homosexual. He was a window blind salesman she dated while she was getting her master's degree in education."

"And did your mother tell you why she thought Charlie Sizer was gay?"

"'Quoting Cher,' he said, 'It was in his kiss.'"

There *was* a sense of humor there, and bonus points for not cracking up at his own joke. If they call that gaining the suspect's trust, Lt. Hailey had mine.

"Shoop shoop," I said, motioning him to take a seat.

Where to start? In April 1984, a month before I graduated from Knox College in Galesburg, Illinois, the Secretary of Health and Human Services reported that AIDS was caused by a retrovirus. It's difficult for people today to understand how terrifying the plague was in its first decade, when the drugs, the few there were, were ineffective and difficult to secure, making a positive diagnosis a certain death sentence.

I decided against joining the local Soangetaha Players for another season of summer stock. Statistically speaking, AIDS hadn't reached West Central Illinois, but potential association with a fresh batch of gay chorus boys might prove too tempting. Hanging around Galesburg after graduation, for even a week, spelled D-E-F-E-A-T. Ditto returning home to my parents in Nebraska until some wisp of a plan, involving combing the classified ads and the generation of an actual resumé—took shape.

A poster in the Knox Career Office caught my eye. Catholic Relief Services was recruiting language majors to volunteer in Africa or Latin America on community infrastructure projects. I'd been raised Catholic, spent a semester in Paris my junior year, and knew nothing of the term infrastructure. My phone interviews, one of them in French, went well. The day before graduation, I had a posting which, given my lack of skills, job experience, and the high unemployment rate of the early Reagan years, seemed miraculous.

With the plague as a warning, and now a year's grace period, I vowed before God to renounce my homosexuality, woo women, conjoin with them, and so forth. I made the mistake of telling this to my best friend, David Towle, also gay, but an extremely devout Catholic virgin. He'd *prepared* for life post-Knox: a free ride to Yale for a doctorate in art history.

"They may come up with a cure before you have to go through all of that," said David.

"I'm doing it for God."

He gave me such a look before saying, "Sénégal is ninety-five percent Muslim."

(That was news.) "Can't a person change his sexual orientation?"

"Just do what's asked of you, and don't fake a faith you don't possess." Over my splutter of protest, David said that just showing up would be enough for God—and Allah—for the time being.

Infrastructure in Sénégal turned out to be babysitting, with a green thumb. Audrey Carrigan of Carleton College '84 and I supervised American high schoolers who spent their days in Ndeundekat helping the locals create a community garden. The students changed over every six weeks. This was long before projects of this kind became part of the calculus used to leverage one's way into a better college or university. These kids wanted to be there, wanted to take part in something larger than themselves; they put me to shame with their unselfconscious references to grace and good works. They required no wrangling. In all of our time in Sénégal, Audrey and I never caught a student with reefer; no one ever bribed a villager for a bottle of rum; no couple was caught necking after lights out; there were no unkind nicknames or designated outcasts. Clearing brush, digging, planting, weeding, and hauling well water nine hours a day in the blistering sun took the cuss out of them. They were an army of cheerful teens with no problems that couldn't be solved by aspirin, calamine lotion, Midol, or Clearasil.

I thought we made an appealing bunch when we walked a mile through the jungle into town from the ramshackle French Colonial mansion where we lodged for Wednesday evening and Sunday morning Masses at the only Catholic church in the district. I led the pack of boys in ties and short-sleeved dress shirts and girls in modest cotton dresses, with my eyes and pointed stick patrolling the trail for black mambas, while Audrey, with a pitch pipe, played caboose. She had grown up idolizing "The Singing Nun," and would lead us in renditions of "Dominique," as well as peppy ecumenical tunes like "Shout from the Highest Mountain" and "Rise and Shine." The village children, on the lookout for us in the packed-earth plaza, would grab our hands and drag us into the pews to sit with their families. There were just enough of us, it seemed, to go around.

Our supervisor, Gunter Vistock, told us not to get swelled heads. Senegalese children believed that white people were magic. I'll admit to misjudging Gunter at the outset. But for the brass crucifix around his neck, he seemed more like an ex-con than a Catholic field rep. A black patch covered his left eye. The bottom half of his left ear had been sheared off. Audrey and I often theorized about Gunter's missing orbit and earlobe. His assailants changed with every surmise, but the conflict always ended in an epic bar fight with animal poachers and bandits.

To maintain his Tarzanesque physique, Gunter lifted weights every day. His first two meals were protein powder mixed with fresh pineapple juice. Dinner was always fish or chicken, with plantains *or* rice, never both, and for dessert, fruit only. Gunter and his tiny, shapely wife, DeeDee, were the first health nuts Audrey and I had ever met. For them, refined sugar was a devil coeval to Satan, an unpopular stance in a country whose second biggest export was sugarcane. On village rounds, Gunter would pluck canes out of the hands and mouths of children and the elderly alike; were it up to him, he would clear the sugar exporters from the harbor market like Jesus at the Temple.

DeeDee Vistock was the village schoolteacher. Her glory was a lustrous mane of red hair that reached to a waist so dainty it seemed to equal Gunter's thigh in circumference. Like the villagers, DeeDee went barefoot, so that when she cinched her hair above her head with an ivory comb, you couldn't help but think of Wilma Flintstone—married to a one-eyed Fred on steroids. Audrey and I dubbed the Vistock children Pebbles and Bamm-Bamm. They looked to be six or seven; we were too shy to ask them, or DeeDee or Gunter, whether they were actual twins.

✳

Lt. Hailey uncrossed his legs and interrupted my monologue. "Pebbles and Bamm-Bamm weren't siblings," he said. Like all expert listeners, he hadn't moved the entire time I'd been speaking.

"You're right," I said. "Bamm-Bamm was the Rubble child."

"They eventually got married in a spin-off."

"I'm not surprised." I glanced at the wall clock behind Lt. Hailey's head. *Uff da ishtah*, as they say in the Dakotas. "Sorry to be going on like this. Professional hazard."

"No worries, Roger," he answered. "But aren't you burying the lede?"

"What lede? Am I on tape?" I asked, worried again. "Am I under investigation?"

He shook his head, held up empty hands. "I'm part of a team doing a background check on Audrey Carrigan."

"For what purpose?"

I let him ignore this direct question. The ebbing sun was throwing onto his legs a harlequinade pattern through the stained glass of my bay window. Once Audrey had let me try on that skirt of hers. It hung from my narrow hips like an empty toilet paper roll. For good measure, she put on one of my white A-shirts, popped a breast around each arm strap, then shook them like a dust mop before we fell into bed.

"Lady C. and I loved to make each other laugh—I can tell you that much."

That might have doomed us. In my experience, only one member in a long-term heterosexual couple is allowed to be funny. I opened the bottom desk drawer and pulled out the Maker's Mark. I set the bottle on the desk and tilted its neck his way. I located shot glasses with two fingers and waited.

"As long as you're pouring," he said.

With a pocket handkerchief [another bonus point] drawn from his suit jacket, he wiped the dust out of his Haverford glass and peered at the insignia. "What's your school mascot?"

"The black squirrel."

"Interesting," he replied. "You don't see many of them."

"I know."

Audrey Carrigan had grown up in Minnesota, the youngest of six children of the town barber. Her parents had met as Catholic missionaries in Sudan; Audrey's mother referred to their two years in the Upper Nile as the kind of romantic adventure everyone should make but unlike the Vistocks, they waited to return to America before having children. It was Audrey's theory that her father had peaked in Africa. Stateside, he became a man overeager to prove his worth, a basement tinkerer with patents pending, as well as an easy touch for sharpers. One time he had converted the family assets into South African krugerrands, then for eighteen months couldn't change them back, long enough for them to lose sixty percent of their value. To keep food on the table, Eileen Carrigan was postmistress, village notary and auctioneer, sold real estate, Mary Kay, and peppermint candy Christmas wreaths.

Audrey made comedy from this material the way I drew laughs from the serial adventures of *Roger the Prairie Pansy*. The pain underneath was a binding agent. We were possibly too sensitive to one another to go the distance as a genuine couple.

Sensitivity wasn't a quality in Audrey's college boyfriends. There had been "*Omoo* Man," an English major with a pretentious preference for Melville's shorter works. There was "Deluxor," who kept handy a box of French ticklers he'd ordered from a *Playboy* ad bearing the imperishable tagline, "Thousands of Tiny Pleasure Dots Urging a Woman to Let Go."

There was "Peter Purdah," who wouldn't so much as hold Audrey's hand on the days of her period, which he had blocked out in marker on his desk calendar. *Uff da*, indeed.

Presently, there was "Bismarck," or Bradley Brennan, an ag ec major from North Dakota. Bismarck maintained a *que sera sera* attitude about everything, including Audrey's spell of service learning in Africa. She wrote him Aerograms twice a week.

One night, after turning out the lights on our charges, separated by sex and one floor of the old mansion, we'd gone up to her room with bottles of Bitter Lemon and a bag of crisps. We lit two candles, then watched the shadows they cast on the wall, flickering from a steady breeze through her louvered windows. Despite the strict "no canoodling" clause in our JVC contracts, we stretched ourselves out along her bed. I was contemplating a first pass when Audrey sat up to pluck a photo from the drawer of the rickety nightstand on her side of the bed.

"What do you think, Roger," she asked.

Bismarck was a sleepy-eyed charmer, with a lopsided smile.

"Is it a good likeness, Lady C?" (That was one of my nicknames for her.)

She rolled her eyes. "Yes, he looks like that."

"He's sexy, but he's straight, if that's what you're worried about."

"I'm *not*," she said, but added quickly, "How can you tell?"

"His hair covers his ears," I said.

Because no one in her Carleton acquaintance had been out and proud, I was the first bisexual Audrey had met. She knew that I had slept with men, emphasis on "in my past." I tactfully—or strategically—didn't detail my intimate connections the way she kept me in stitches with her suite of swains. That she was sexually experienced and didn't play the Catholic missionary was part of her initial hold on me. Had we both been virgins, we might have popped out a child or two and stayed on in the bush as Barney and Betty Rubble. Kids having kids was environmental in Sénégal. Some of the local women pitching in with the garden project would pepper Audrey with questions to that effect. Several no older than our high schoolers would scare the bejesus out of her whenever they'd point to their offspring nearby and wonder, in so many words, when she was going to obey her biological imperative. I was never consulted. Men, mere seed-sowers, were beside the point.

We had been outside of Ndeundekat for six weeks when something weird happened, an incident that became routine every night before the student changeover. Audrey, in full *Singing Nun* mode, was teaching the refrain of our French translation of *This Land is Your Land* to our kids. We'd be teaching it to the villagers the next day during a farewell *fête d'adieu* before the students left by van for Dakar. After herding them on their charter flight to DC, Audrey and I would have thirty-six free hours in the capital before we collected the next round of do-gooders:

C'est notre terre
C'est votre terre
Car il ne reste plus de frontière,
Tant d'amitié
Tant de bonheur
Nous ne vous oublierons jamais.

Audrey was leading the altos when Gunter appeared in the doorway of the common room. He made a motion to stop rehearsal and send the kids to bed, not a problem since his presence terrified them. He lowered his flashlight and said he'd wait.

When we came back down, DeeDee was by his side, holding the hand of a little girl who was wearing a dark *ibadou* with a white *hijab*.

"This is Noor," said Gunter, more to Audrey than to me. "She needs to leave with you for Dakar tomorrow."

"What's wrong?" I asked.

Gunter ignored me. "Keep her with you, Audrey, and see if some of the girls can lend her some clothes. And a baseball cap."

"She needs to look American," said DeeDee. She crouched and slid her arm around the girl's waist. "Écoute, Noor. Voilà Mademoiselle Audrey. Elle est gentille, et elle va bien prendre soin de toi. N'aie pas peur, ma mignonne. Tout le monde est très fièr de toi."

Noor put a hand to her mouth.

"Won't she be recognized in the village?" I asked.

"She's not from here," said Gunter, again cutting me off.

"Je m'appelle Roger," I said to Noor, who wouldn't look at me all the time she was under our care. I hoped it was cultural.

Audrey was so preoccupied with Noor the next day that I was left to teach "C'est Notre Terre" and make merry with the villagers. Neither task was a special skill, so I was already in a bad mood when we set off for Dakar. Audrey's refusal to disclose any details about what I was beginning to consider a purloined child, plus the constant chirp of the students closing out their African adventure, made it worse. The last straw was the driver dropping Noor *and* Audrey off in front of a nondescript, whitewashed house on the outskirts of the capital, a turn of events that left me in charge of the passports, the tickets, the money exchange, the luggage, *every last fricking damn thing* at the airport.

When we met up again, at the ferry that was to take us offshore to the House of Slaves (or enslaved persons) Museum, I was fuming. I had overpacked my duffel, and I needed a shower; Audrey, by contrast, was the picture of a composed Good Samaritan, a paisley weekender in repose at her feet. I should mention that Lady C. was as beautiful as she was funny. Her straight chestnut hair was long enough to tuck just so behind her ears; her nose tilted upwards but stopped short of being snub; she had a broad forehead, a wicked smile, and skin like you'd squeezed an eyedropper of cherry juice into a pail of milk.

"You could have warned me that I was going to have to run the entire show," I snarled, resisting the urge to kick the bench.

"I'm happy to see you too," she laughed.

"So what's the deal with Noor? Is she escaping a forced marriage or something?"

"It's worse than that."

"What could—"

"You don't want to know, Roger," replied Audrey, handing up her bottle of beer for me to finish. "Trust me." Her topaz eyes were glistening.

"Okay, then."

I had to have a second round before she could get me to admit that I had enjoyed mastering all the chores of the day. No one had missed the plane, lost a passport, or left luggage behind.

You know how they say that the news of a death in the family begets a need in the survivors to create life? This will sound wrong, and it's the kind of admission my social justice warrior students at Haverford would string me up for, but our visit to the Maison des Esclaves on the Île de Gorée was the catalyst for Audrey and me having sex for the first time. It was a late 18th-century colonial manor house, similar to our decaying dorm upcountry, that had become a deportation center during the Atlantic slave trade. More than fifteen million captured Africans had been chained in airless basement barracoons before being forced onto ships bound for the Americas.

Audrey broke down several times on the tour. I managed to keep it together until our guide, Boubacar Ndiaye, who had himself founded the museum in 1962, led us to "The Door of No Return." The Atlantic Ocean was sparkling in the afternoon sun when Boubacar, to drive home his final point, picked up and rattled a pair of iron shackles.

We held each other on the ferry back to town, then clasped hands over the table through a drunken West African meal whose spices helped keep our tear ducts flowing. We were drained when we got back to the Catholic Services hostel in the center of town. After a chaste goodnight, I lay down on my cot in my cubicle. After fifteen minutes or so, I nerved up, knocked on Audrey's door down the hall, and she welcomed me into her cot.

I felt in alien territory, not having touched any part of a woman since an acting class in high school, but my penis knew where it wanted to be. As I learned what a woman's body was like, we were intimate in a careful, considered way. Audrey was friendly and laughing and so very soft and full. What puzzled me most was her telling me what felt nice. I knew everything about men, or imagined I did, but had no conception of what her pleasure might feel like, or what might cause it. That first night, I thought of my father off and on, wondering whether this physical distance was a mystery that we shared as men, or one that he had solved with my mother.

When we returned to the village the next day with our second batch of teenagers, we continued a relationship known today as "friends with benefits." We always used my room for sex. She would slip out in the morning before the girls got up downstairs. We took more time; I learned some maneuvers; I learned how to hold back; Audrey's casual approach, and her capacity for play kept me from overthinking; she continued to beseech Bismarck by Aerogram. I wrote David in New Haven about my official bisexuality. The unreal yet utterly real tropical surroundings and the pleasures of making things grow out of the earth kept thoughts of my future on hold.

Audrey had a suggestion one night. "You know, we could do this more than once each time, Roger."

My eyes popped open as if a cartoon coconut had dropped on my head. Call me naïve—or grotesquely selfish—but I had not felt the need to do it again, had not suspected that she might want me to. Recalling the marathon all-night ruts I'd had with men, nights when my mind took a backseat to my body, and time stood still, I began to blush. Then, of course, I realized Audrey had experienced her own wild nights (to borrow from Emily Dickinson), with or without thousands of tiny pleasure dots.

One and done—could anything be more gay?

"Do you want me to?" I asked.

"Well...."

Our last few times, I sincerely tried. Then, when she tried to help me out, I shut down completely. It is a universal truth that Roger Hauf needs to test well. I was a fraudulent heterosexual who would never be good enough to satisfy a woman in the sack. It was as simple—and at the time, as shaming—as that.

Lt. Hailey's response to the revelation of my Imposter Syndrome was the kind of *non sequitur* only a straight man would make: "Do you know that historians have since debunked the number of Africans who passed through "The Door of No Return" at the Maison des Esclaves? From fifteen million to more like twenty-six or so thousand?"

Was that supposed to make me feel better? I wanted to tell Lt. Hailey that suffering was suffering, no matter its extent, but I have learned in the classroom that editorializing, or quantifying, suffering is not a job for the survivors. A white person should think twice today before visiting one of the most infamous barracoons from the transatlantic slave trade. A non-Jew shouldn't visit the Nazi crematoria, and so forth. The term is misery tourism.

I recalled the peanuts and cassava and white sweet potatoes the students and I used to pull from the ground and toss with happy shouts into our plastic tubs. We'd sing while we worked—songs with words like "Lord" and "God" in the lyrics—as enslaved Blacks had in Antebellum South Carolina. Had our Ndeundekat community garden been a positive effort toward human relief, or two shameful acres of misery tourism? I suddenly felt about a million years old.

"Why did you leave Sénégal ahead of schedule, Roger?"

This sudden shift was confusing. What did Washington have on me? I was and am not really that interesting enough a person to take notes on. Moreover, had I not just revealed the worst of it to him? After Audrey Carrigan, I never attempted another intimate relationship with a woman. My vow withered away in the African heat. Lt. Hailey's insinuation that I had abridged my official storyline offended me.

"How is that *germane* to the discussion? Have you talked with Audrey?"

"I can't answer that, Roger."

"Then what's left to tell? Wait—what is that chemical you mentioned when you first came in?"

"Chlordecone."

"Yes. That. What is chlordecone?"

"Chlordecone is a compound similar to DDT, sprayed on bananas. It was outlawed in the United States in the early 1980s after it polluted a major segment of the James River in Virginia. It's still used in parts of the developing world."

His scientific recitation sounded like the climax of a Scooby-Doo mystery.

"What does a chemical compound similar to DDT have to do with my time in Sénégal? We didn't grow bananas, and the only thing we spread on our community garden was horseshit."

"Do you know what Alfred Hitchcock called the McGuffin?"

"Of course I do! I teach dramatic literature, for Christ's sake!"

"After her time in Sénégal, Audrey went to the Caribbean and helped disrupt the legal trade in chlordecone."

From the waning light outside, we had reached, as the Czechs say, the hour between dog and wolf, and landed back at square one: hostile suspicion. Lt. Hailey aggressively ran a thumbnail back and forth on the edge of my desk. He ignored the phone buzzing in his pocket. Was that a pre-arranged signal from headquarters to push me to further confession? I had made my confession.

"Who are you?" I finally asked in a defeated tone. "Whose background are you really checking?"

"Audrey Carrigan is being vetted as a judicial candidate for the Court of Appeals for the Eighth Circuit." Before I could begin to process this change-up, he shifted gears once more. "Did you ever wonder what the Vistocks were doing when they took Noor and the other girls from their families?"

"Audrey never told me, and I didn't push her. What did she know that I didn't?"

Lt. Hailey pressed his fingers together and leaned forward. "Worse than a forced marriage, Roger, is female genital mutilation. It's a not uncommon practice in Muslim Africa."

He let that sink in. Of course, I had been made aware of FGM, but in an academic way, in my academic life. It was the kind of issue Haverford students held rallies about and chalked the sidewalks to promote awareness of. The way my generation had once rallied for financial divestiture in apartheid South Africa.

"Audrey Carrigan stayed in Sénégal for another two years, helping the Vistocks with their clandestine activities."

"Did Catholic Relief know about this?" I asked.

"I'm sure that CRS would not have approved of such a dangerous undertaking."

"It *was* dangerous. They should have shut the Vistocks down. We were all just innocent kids."

"Why you were asked to leave?" Now Lt. Hailey was pissed.

"You said this isn't *my* background check."

"Point taken, but you might as well tell me."

I nodded, relieved, I suppose, to let it all out. "*One* of us was asked to leave."

"Go on, Dr. Hauf."

"Gunter and DeeDee had gone away again and brought back another girl for us to smuggle. After Noor, I had stopped asking their names. On the morning of their return, someone reported having seen Audrey and me in bed together."

"One of the students?"

"I have no idea. I do recall hearing my bedroom door slam shut one night and thinking that it wasn't the wind. Anyway, we owned up to having sex, and Gunter invoked the morals clause. One of us had to go. Audrey wanted to stay. I pleaded with her to leave too, but she said that I was being selfish, and that Africa and the Vistocks needed her more than I did."

(That was also when she said, while all of Mboro Ndeundekat was warbling "C'est notre terre, c'est votre terre," that I was really gay, and that she couldn't save me.)

"Gunter gave me ten minutes to throw everything into my duffel, plus a wad of bills for a plane ticket. I never saw him or DeeDee again."

My goodbye to Audrey was in the van, idling in front of the house on the city outskirts; the hopped-up students in contrast to the girl, her *hijab* under a baseball cap, her shoulders circled in Audrey's arms.

"You made the right choice," said Lt. Hailey.

"Who the fuck asked you for your opinion?"

That just flew out of my mouth.

"My parents couldn't trust you the way they trusted Audrey."

"Your parents?"

He nodded.

Holy shit. "You're...?" I nearly said Bamm-Bamm.

"My birth name is Benjamin."

"Not Benedict?"

"Benjamin. That's French for—"

"The younger, or youngest child," I said.

"My sister, Sofia, and I were born fourteen months apart.

"Irish twins then," trying for humor. "Why do you go by Hailey?

"I took my mother's maiden name after my father lost his life."

I didn't know how to react, except to pour him the last of the bourbon.

In 1987, a year after Audrey Carrigan had left Sénégal, Gunter was attempting another rescue, this time in a village perilously close to Ndeundekat. At this point, he and DeeDee, and in-the-know CRS volunteers, had prevented twenty-three girls, ages twelve to fourteen, from genital infibulation. This time he was ambushed by the women from the girl's own family. They used machetes. He tried to make it home but collapsed and bled out fifty yards from their compound. Sofia found his body and lost the ability to speak for almost a decade.

The remaining Vistocks were airlifted out of the country and sent to live with DeeDee's family in North Carolina. Benjamin went into the Foreign Service after UNC Chapel Hill, returned to America after postings in the Middle East, and had been living ten miles from his mother in Rockville, Maryland. Sofia got married, divorced, and went back to the bush to continue her parents' work in Burkina Faso, this time in a non-clandestine NGO dedicated to preventing FGM.

I leaned in, hoping to find traces of his parents in Benjamin's face, but of course, I couldn't. I'd known Gunter and DeeDee a mere six months. "Where did the rescued girls go?"

"They took them to a safe house, with a school. They only took girls whose mothers and aunts wanted them to escape their fate."

"Doesn't your investigation present a conflict of interest?"

"I asked for this case specifically, Roger."

That I understood. The older I get, the more I believe that solving the mystery of one's parents is a universal need. I straightened up in my chair. "Don't take this the wrong way..." I began.

"What?"

"What happened to your father's eye?"

"That was his first warning—in Mali, where we were posted before Sénégal—that his ideas about female autonomy went against local customs."

"And his ear?"

"My mother has never told me. She may not know herself. As a boy, I pictured an epic bar fight. With crashing chairs. The way you and Audrey had."

My mind, swimming for some time now with tragic and absurd associations, suddenly remembered that Audrey had found Gunter sexy, a fact I had repressed when we were intimate together. I had never revealed that I agreed with her. Gunter Vistock was hot—a hot, ragged-ear rogue do-gooder, as it turned out. There were probably nights when we both fantasized that we were in bed with him. Tracking my forehead with my fingers, I again felt ancient. Since Audrey had stayed on another two years, aiding and abetting the Vistock underground railroad, I asked Benjamin whether he thought his father and Audrey had ever slept together.

He drained his already empty shot glass. He began checking pockets in his suit jacket, as if his phone had dematerialized, and then reached down to tug up one sock, then the other, all gestures that meant my impertinent question had never crossed his mind.

"I was ten when he died, Roger."

"Was killed," I wanted to say, but it wasn't my story.

"If they did, I never caught them at it."

He leaned back in his chair, crossed his arms, and looked down at me with a glint in his eye. The way he'd caught Audrey and me once upon a time. His parents must have left Pebbles and Bamm-Bamm in our care in the manor house while they went to fetch the last girl.

There was no need for us to corroborate this final piece of the puzzle. Once a spy, always a spy. "Touché," I said.

Given how truth and memory were playing tricks, I asked him whether Audrey herself was another McGuffin, designed to throw me off the trail of some larger, cosmological answer that he, or the Pentagon, was seeking.

"I told you she's being vetted for the Court of Appeals for the Eighth Circuit."

My mind blipped to an easy question. "Which one is the Eighth?"

"It's a basic straight shot from Minnesota down through Arkansas. Plus, the Dakotas."

I visualized Minneapolis to Little Rock in a covered wagon, or on a Mississippi River steamboat, or on foot, with a backpack and a baseball cap to ward off the sun. *C'est notre terre, c'est votre terre, car il ne reste plus de frontière...*

All these journeys we set off on, with no clear destination. Rounded with a sleep, as Prospero says. I was getting maudlin, and his stomach was growling. I pictured a harlequin skirt playing peekaboo underneath judicial robes. "Do you think that these youthful activities will help or hurt Audrey's confirmation chances in the Senate?"

He hesitated. "I agree that Audrey Carrigan is a woman of quality. And her activities were those of a woman of quality. But I just gather information and file a report."

"Really?"

"And truly."

It made me sad that Lt. Benjamin Dailey held no more power than that. No, it made me sad that our combined history held no more power than that. I looked around my office, its shapes suspended now in shadow: couch, dictionary stand, coat rack, clock, Windsor chair, a dusty plant on the embrasure, an empty bourbon bottle. On the wall, Henrik Ibsen, pilloried in his lifetime, stood as an eternal force for good. If told the tale, my students might easily cancel Gunter Vistock for being a White Savior, and a man to boot, but I know in my heart that during his time on earth, he had been a force for good. I felt certain that DeeDee, whom her son had rung up to kick off our bizarre, latter-day encounter, remained a force for good. Audrey Carrigan was, and Sofia too. Why not me? Why not—if provided the opportunity—everybody?

We stood at the same time. I extended my hand.

"Sorry for your loss, Benjamin."

"Friends call me 'Benny.'"

We shook on it, and he was gone.

Sister Essence, Princess Of Hope

For Janice Kotte Stariha (1961-2022)

My brother, Bud, emailed that he'd taken our mother to the doctor. She'd been complaining off and on in the last year of forgetfulness. The doctor administered a standard cognitive test, and she scored eighteen out of thirty. The diagnosis was mild or early dementia.

E.F.—who had managed the decline, fall, and burial of both of his parents—made me feel a little better when he said that these results weren't final; she might just as easily score twenty-four on the MMSE (Mini Mental State Examination) the next time she took it.

I called home. My father was typically sanguine. "This explains why she's been getting the sixes and nines mixed up in dominoes." My mother started her end of our conversation by reminding me of the prayer she's said every night for the last longest: "Please send me home, Lord, in my right mind, in my own bed."

"We should all be so lucky, Mom."

"I'm eighty-six, Roger. I've had a rich, full life.

"You make it sound like a cup of coffee."

When I promised to come home as soon as I could, she accused me of overreacting.

✳

I shuffled some class meetings, but E.F. was on call the first week of December; my mother couldn't hide her disappointment when I showed up alone. "I was hoping there'd be someone to braid my hair in the mornings," she said, looking past me to see whether he might not be getting out of the rental car anyway. Things go better in Nebraska when E.F. is along. If I thought about it too much, I'd say my mother would be happy to turn back the clock fifty years and have a crack at keeping him straight. I have yet to convince her entirely that I didn't "turn" E.F. in a vulnerable moment.

"Why is your hair so long, Mom?" It was scrunched at the back of her head like an untidy dryer ball.

"My shoulder is frozen, so I can't reach up to do anything nice with it anymore."

"You could get it cut."

She made a face. Call her Samson. Or Richard O'Brien as Riff Raff in the film version of *The Rocky Horror Picture Show,* which is how she looked the next morning—without makeup, in sleep sweats, her straight, fine hair halfway down her back—when we crossed paths on the way to the bathroom. With her hormones at a low ebb, she nearly presented as a man, which was disturbing. I studied my father at the breakfast table; he had been a looker too, but time had worn the planes and edges in his face to womanly curves and pouches, his neck not dissimilar from the dried gourds he made into birdhouses in his workroom off the garage.

Spending time with them, those four days in North Platte, I felt little had changed in the big picture. They were closer to one another on the gender spectrum, but they shared the same bed, and their senses of humor were intact. Like old men the world over, my father joined a group of ballcapped buddies at the Hardee's every morning to shoot the shit over endless refills, and my mother talked about the same ten pounds she's wanted to lose since 1975. Bud, who checked in on them twice a week, had installed rails and bathroom grips in the rancher they'd moved into post-retirement. A plus to their downsizing had been the evaporation of my adolescent bedroom, a queer boy's hope chest theretofore preserved in amber. Next to a poster of Sandy Dennis, an early screen obsession, in *Up the Down Staircase,* I had tacked favorite covers from my *New Yorker* subscription onto Day-Glo corkboard rectangles. Pride of place on my nightstand was a framed, signed glossy from The Manhattan Transfer singing group. That, I had thought, would be my life's trajectory—a permanent transfer to the Tuxedo Junction called New York City.

✳

That I had had no friends to bring home to this minty den of mine was the mythology, but Monday morning at Great Plains Health, the Neurology Intake Coordinator provided a corrective with a squeal and swing around her desk.

"Roger Hauf, is that really you?" she said, hugging my midsection. "Jolly Roger? My word, it's great to see you!"

My nickname at North Platte High had been Jolly Roger, a British naval reference to male-on-male intercourse. Jolly for short, or Jolly Boy, or the occasional Jollipop. Because the girls were in on it too, the name-calling could sometimes feel worse than all the bruises, welts, split lips, and pink bellies I'd receive from a roving squad of athlete-sadists.

"It's good to see you too," I said, scanning for a name tag, or a desk plate. "This is my mother, Evelyn."

"No need to tell me. She's a favorite patient here."

"That's wonderful," I said. "Well. How have *you* been all these years?"

She drooped back to her chair. "You don't recognize me?"

Hands over heart, I shook my head. "I'm sorry. I know we were in high school together. But that was forty-some years ago."

"How about a hint?"

I shrugged okay.

Clicking my mother's details into her monitor, the woman began a speech: "So anyway, I married the S.O.B. I had it all planned out. First, he'd take over the History Department, then when Daddy retired, he'd take over the whole college, you know. That was the way it was supposed to be, getting angry baby, huh?"

Here, she looked directly at me. Was it my line?

She continued a mocking, needling recital. "And Daddy thought it was a good idea too. For a while. Until he started watching for a couple of years—getting angrier?" She handed my mother a printout and a pen and kept going. I admired her multitasking.

"Daddy started watching and thinking that maybe it wasn't such a good idea after all, that maybe Georgie Boy didn't have the stuff."

'Georgie Boy' was the tip-off. She was quoting Martha in *Who's Afraid of Virginia Woolf?* a play I had taught in my American drama course before it started triggering too many of my Haverford students from fractured homes.

She tilted her head and drew my mother in. "You see, George didn't have much *push*. He wasn't particularly aggressive. In fact, he was sort of a FLOP!" She took a breath. "A GREAT BIG FAT FLOP!!!!"

I slammed my fist on the counter and shouted, "Stop it, Martha!"

My mother jumped. Sense memory, they call it.

"I hope that was an empty bottle, George," she snarled. "You can't afford to waste good liquor. Not on an *associate* professor's salary."

And—scene. The woman traded my mother's paper and pen for a beeper to signal her when the doctor would be ready, then began hooting with laughter.

"Robin Elfstrom?" I said. "Holy hell, that can't be you!"

"It is!"

"No."

"Except I'm Robin Kees now."

Our embrace, take two, was genuine and reciprocal. I asked her how she remembered all those lines.

"Never hear of the Internet, *Swampy*?"

When we were juniors at North Platte High, Robin Elfstrom and I had been in Acting I, taught by Miss Kulinski, an enthusiastic new hire whose stated mission was to shake the dust off the Performing Arts Department. We were to call her Merle, in the familiar way of theater artists. Acting I was largely an off-load for untouchables, but we had a couple of cheerleaders in class, and even a few good-looking jocks who must have fantasized, deep down, that they were the next Robert Redford or Paul Newman. (*Butch Cassidy and the Sundance Kid* and *The Sting* were huge at the time.)

Merle's first innovation was axing the annual "Pawnee Pageant," a fall semester talent show that traditionally—and I mean, here was a tradition that had stretched back *decades*—climaxed with the varsity football team

performing a pom-pom routine in full drag, to "I Enjoy Being a Girl."
Merle replaced it with an ambitious "Evening of Scenes" from Acting I:
twenty minutes apiece from *Who's Afraid of Virginia Woolf?*, *Butterflies
are Free*, and *The Lion in Winter*. Everyone campaigned to play the
hippie chick, Jill, classifiable today as a vintage Manic Pixie Dream Girl,
and Don, the blind boy who gets to strum his guitar and sing his title
tune in *Butterflies are Free*. I hoped to play Geoffrey, the overlooked
middle prince in *The Lion in Winter,* but Merle, reading my sixteen-year-
old beads, cast me as a second-rate academic whose balls are on
permanent roll between his wife's canines. (To be fair, George has
Martha over her own dramaturgical barrel.)

I didn't remember who played Nick and Honey with us, but Robin
did…and then some. As my mother and I waited for Dr. Williams' signal,
she unspooled the fates of dozens of teachers and classmates she thought
I might recall. Her interest in the minutiae of their lives made me think
of Herodotus, Hesiod, Clotho, Froissart, and the great 18th-century
Encylopédistes. The smooth ribbon of her chronicle began to instill in me
an odd sensation: I was becoming homesick for a North Platte I'd never
been to, for a magical place I hadn't appreciated, or even deserved to hail
from. (The Germans call this feeling *Heimweh*.)

But you know what? Bullshit. North Platte High had been a misery;
I'd fled ASAP, never to return, no forwarding address. *Heimweh* was an
absurdly pretentious way to stanch the seepage from forty-year-old
gashes. That "Evening of Scenes" had tanked, and the school board
ordered the reinstatement of the Pawnee Pageant, wigs, eyelashes, and all,
for the following semester. My commitment to playing George might
have demonstrated an affinity for the stage, but it also provided fresh
ammo to the Roger Hauf Extermination Squad. They added "FLOP!"
and "Swampy," "Angel Tits" and "Monkey Nipples," to the "Jolly Roger"
roll call. They reinterpreted my manly smash of the liquor bottle as an
effete, pinky-up cracking of an egg. They hailed me wherever and
whenever with a protracted, Charles Nelson Reilly-ish "Ssssssstop it,
Martha!" Those twenty minutes of Albee may have been instrumental to
my future as a scholar of dramatic form, but decades later, listening to
Robin's recap, a tsunami of sense memories was making me flush, pit out
my undershirt, and breathe through my mouth like a cornered animal.
So much so that, when she invited me to come out the next night to hear

her do stand-up at an open mic event at the River's Edge Golf Course—
"a bunch of the 'old gang' would be there"—I felt close to puking.

Gang was right. I dabbed the moisture beading along my hairline with
a tissue yanked from a metal box welded to the table. My mother clapped
her hands and said that was a wonderful idea. Seconding Robin's insane
proposition was the abrupt beep and flash of the monitor in her lap. I
wanted to dive through a window and put out my flames in a snowbank,
but the best I could do was hustle the old Judas and her pocketbook into
the examining room.

"It'll be so much fun!" said Robin.

The upside to Monday morning: my mother scored twenty-two on
an MMSE do-over. The downside: the flyer and free beer chit Robin
Kees pressed upon me as we left the neurology bay.

✳

E.F. thought I should go but didn't insist.

"High school is over, Roger," he said on the phone. E.F.'s years at the
all-male St. Ig's in Baltimore had been trauma-free.

"High school is *never* over," I countered.

"Have it your way," he said mildly. "But if this girl you once knew is
brave enough to do stand-up comedy, why can't you be brave enough to
go listen and support her?"

"You are so fired," I said, not for the first time.

✳

They had completely done over the River's Edge Golf Course clubhouse.
The Queen Anne edifice, which I had found so stylishly "Nantucket" as
a swirly teenager, was gone, replaced by a three-story, gambrel-roofed
brick pile with, in deference to car culture, a seemingly endless portico of
flagstone columns. It looked like a cross between a tobacco plantation
and a suburban steakhouse. The parking lot seemed to have doubled in
size, and they had wisely removed the fiberglass wigwam where the
stoned valets had stored the car keys and hung out back in the day.

To the left in the lobby, the seasonal decorations were restrained: origami snowflakes and holly bushes in the urns under an enfilade of portraits of the corn and sorghum baron founders of the club that led to Morningwood, a members-only, fine dining experience. To the right, a jagged hell mouth of blinking neon arrows dripped tinsel and pointed me to my destination, "Another Round"—a combination bar, stage, casual eatery, and playpen for the rambunctious of all ages and creeds. The marketing made demographic sense. Country club memberships have fallen off a cliff.

Inside "Another Round," as predicted, was a surplus of flat-screen TVs to vex my spirit with sports coverage. Behind the host station were headshots of the five comics for the night. I couldn't place Robin's photo at first. Her hair, dark and shoulder-length at Great Plains Health, was now piled high in a brassy red bouffant, anchored in the center with a big black bow, like Minnie Mouse, or Rose Marie on *The Dick Van Dyke Show*. The curl to her lip suggested a cigarette in her unseen hand. Very Martha, I thought, then hoped to God she wouldn't try to drag me and George into her set; comics are wicked improvisers.

I asked to be seated far from the stage. The hostess put me at a high two-top in a back corner. To avoid company, I draped my heavy coat over the second chair.

The room looked about a third full. "Not bad for a Tuesday," I said.

"Give it an hour. We'll be packed to the rafters," she said, handing me a laminated menu.

"Why is that?"

"It's Karaoke Night." My stomach lurched, and not just at the lurid images of Buffalo wings and loaded potato skins in my hands. "Greta will come by in a minute for your drink order."

Before things got too sensitive on campus, I used to joke with my theater majors that there were three things I would go to my grave without ever doing: karaoke, LSD, and paying for sex. (The most puckish would respond that if I started with the acid, I could score three-for-three in the same night.) Just being in a venue where karaoke happened creeped me out. Its ubiquitous spread in the 1990's was unfathomable. My oldest friend, David Towle, once pointed out that I had had no problem singing solos in summer stock. I'd counter that it was easy to sing as somebody else—Motel the Tailor in *Fiddler on the Roof,* etc., but nothing could be more terrifying than to stand and sing *as myself* before a crowd of strangers.

I used my beer chit and, given my bias that comedy nights were a heterosexual pursuit, I ate my chicken-fried steak with the wariness of an interloper. (Karaoke once belonged in this category, but young queers of every gender can't get enough of it.) I avoided all eye contact.

The five comics filed in and sat in a row behind the microphone with their water bottles. Robin's fireball bouffant caught the light as she shaded her eyes to scan the house. There was enough of the old gang, whoever they were, for her to wave to.

Most of the comedy was, predictably, joke-centered; Nebraska winters; Cornhuskers football; swipes at Omahans, etc. I managed a chuckle at a woman's expletive-laden, mimed struggle to open a plastic grocery store produce bag, and I laughed in agreement to an older guy's riff on how the replacement of bar soap with shower gels and body washes was one more sign of irreversible, millennial decline.

During his applause, Robin, going last, sprang up and took instant control with the mic.

"Greetings North Platte," she said. "If you see me around town during the day, I answer to the name of Robin Kees, devoted wife of Daniel Boone Kees, and bewildered mother to Kayla, Christopher, and Nancy Kees, but come the nighttime"—she paused for some applause—"Come the nighttime"—cheers now—"I'm—go on, say it if you know it, say it like you mean it, say it like my life depends on it, because it does, I'm—"

"Sister Essence!" shouted some people in the crowd.

"That's right, I'm Sister Essence!"

And here Robin whisked off her wig and tossed it behind her. It snagged for a second against the brick wall, then fell to the floor, where it lay like a napping fox.

There were gasps from the uninitiated—like me—but also whistles, and louder cheers. Sister Essence had a following.

"Submit yourselves to Sister Essence, the Cancer Lady!"

The contrast between Robin's bald head and her overdone eye makeup, brows, and plum blush was like a George Grosz lithograph.

Instead of jokes, Robin's routine was a schema. At lightning speed, so fast that it was hard to release for laughter, she performed a literal alphabet of her health saga.

'A' was for acceptance. Well, she was standing here in front of us tonight, wasn't she?

'B' was for breasts. She described her "girls," Connie and Bonnie Elfstrom, two pleasure centers who had cruelly turned on her in 2004. She riffed about their lifetime of shifting sizes, about weaning her reluctant son from his snack bar; she joked about having to "cut them dead" with Obamacare, then imitated her husband's expression when he first saw the mastectomy scars.

'C' was neither a list of carcinogens, nor chemotherapy. C was compassion, a quality she'd found in short supply, even from her oldest and dearest, who basically couldn't believe her cancer was happening to THEM. "Compassion is not a pie," she concluded, "with limited slices." That drew applause.

'D' was for dryness—her mouth, her nasal passages, her hair before it fell out, her vagina, nicknamed Death Valley until she'd found the right lubricant.

Her command to submit to her was correct, as on she went, with spellbinding bravery. Some letters landed better than others, but she hooked us all. No one coughed, or sneezed, took a bite, or rattled their ice. It wasn't stand-up; it was performance art.

'H,' for Hope, was my favorite. To the best of my recollection, Robin said, "My hope doesn't have feathers, like that goddam poem from high school. That kind of hope you can take out of the sky with an air rifle? Nope. Not for Sister Essence. My hope has bristles, and a snout, and a fierce, huge way about him, a way that will roll over and kill you before it takes death for an answer, because my hope, ladies, gentlemen, and everybody, is a 700-pound Javelina Hog, who answers to the name of LIFE!"

Here she paused for cheers, a swig of water, then before we were ready, jumped into 'I' for intubation. 'M' was for metastases. Two years ago, her cancer, whom she had named Chinchilla DeVere, had come a-creepin' back as delicate shadows on her bones. Now her CAT scans looked like lace tablecloths, and her brain was getting mighty nervous about having a date with Chinchilla in about six months, ten months if she got lucky.

'P' was for prayer. "I want you to know that Sister Essence says her prayers every night—for the planet, for climate change, for the senseless wars going on all over, for all of her brothers and sisters fighting something real bad and real hard, and finally, she prays for herself, saying "Dear Lord, please send me home, in my right mind, in my own bed."

Had she learned that from my mother? Before I'd left the house for River's Edge, my mother hadn't let on that she knew the first thing about Robin Kees, or her comedy act.

'R' was Radiology; 'X' was an X-ray tech named Carlos who raced her motor; 'Y' was Yellow.

"And 'Z'?" she said. She waited in a charged silence.

"Well folks, I change 'Z' up every time I get up here, you know, just to keep all y'all guessing. Can someone out there guess what 'Z' stands for tonight?"

She drained the last of her water bottle, then produced a hankie and mopped the sweat on her head. She mimed wringing it out into a patron's beer mug in the front row.

"Zebra!" shouted someone.

She laughed. "Come on, you can do better than that. Zebra was months ago."

She nixed Zeppelin, zoo, zap, and Zeus. As for zippers, hadn't she'd already covered her mastectomy scars?

'Z,' she finally revealed, was for 'Zounds.'

Sister Essence said she wouldn't be able to finish her set until someone released her with the meaning of 'zounds.' Because I knew the meaning, I had the nutty idea that she was directing 'zounds' to me. I recalled a long-ago lunch hour when we were rehearsing *Virginia Woolf* by ourselves and, aware of what it took for me to survive a single day at North Platte High School, Robin told me that my gifts were too big for Nebraska. The surge of gratitude and affection I began to feel for my former, ailing scene partner was cut short by a young woman down in front who cheated by reading the definition of 'zounds' from her smartphone: "A medieval oath, expressing surprise or anger. An abbreviation for "by God's wounds."

"By God's wounds" was Sister Essence's closer. God submitted to the wounds and the sins of the world so that we might all have everlasting life in Him. She quoted John 3:16 ("For God so loved the world...etc.") and thanked us all for our support.

During the prolonged ovation, I reasoned that Robin's faith was helping her stay alive, but it was also what kept Sister Essence from the wider audience she deserved—on the comedy club circuit, or maybe a shot at late-night television, then maybe a stocking stuffer book of wisdom. Proximity had blanked my critical sensors, but that's what the best live performances do to us.

It was time to flee "Another Round." I'd congratulate Robin, refrain from telling her that she had "killed," and give her my email address so we could please please please stay in touch. But once they'd opened the doors, seventy-five people rushed in for karaoke, half of them in a beeline to the stage for sign-up.

Robin retrieved her wig in the melee, settled it back on her head, then wheeled out the karaoke machine, topped by an enormous binder of sheet music. She would be our hostess. Why was I not surprised?

✳

As the merchants say on home shopping shows, "But wait, there's more."

People were eyeing the empty seat beside me. I plucked up my coat and was ready to fight my way through the mob to blow a farewell kiss to Robin when a man, his hand extended, stopped me.

"Roger Hauf?"

Shit. An Old Gang-ster. "Yes," I answered.

"Robin said you'd be here tonight."

"That's great," I said, vaguely. He didn't look familiar, but neither had she. I'd erased them all from my hard drive.

The man dropped his hand. "I'm Robin's radiologist. Matthew Pedrick."

"That's not possible," I said instantly. "That's just not possible."

He sat down. "Sit, Roger."

Having obeyed Matt Pedrick in the past—or else—I sat, using my coat as a shield in case he had a fresh punch to throw. It wasn't possible that this person was Matt Pedrick, the second cruelest of my tormenters at North Platte High. (Cruelest was Bob Farber.) Time had fleshed him out; he'd lost much of his hair; he was a generic, placid-looking, middle-aged man. He signaled the waitress.

"I wouldn't have thought you'd become a doctor," I finally said.

"You think ex-jocks sell insurance, or cars."

"Or they teach gym."

He rapped his hand on the table. An involuntary flinch sent my coat to the floor. He had a clear shot, but instead of a punch to my gut, he asked me what I was drinking. I was too flustered to respond. He ordered a Heineken, and I mumbled, "Same for me."

Matt held my gaze with slightly popped, bright blue eyes. Wolf eyes. His rounded features reminded me of the changes in my father; I could only remember a tight face held in an angry scrunch inches from mine, with a raised fist for follow-through. It was inches away again, but affable this time, almost beseeching.

Who doesn't wish to confront (and ideally, slay) one's oppressor? Many and many a night, I had licked my wounds in my lair, listening to the number flaps race away in the clock radio on my nightstand while plotting revenge on Matt Pedrick and Bob Farber.

"Wow," I said, shaking my head.

"I heard you went east, Roger," he said. "I heard you'd become a teacher."

"A college professor. Theater. Drama."

"That makes sense."

His chuckle here—as if mercilessly mocking my George in *Who's Afraid of Virginia Woolf* was part of *his* plan for *my* future success—sprang the lock. He must have known it was coming, or why was he sitting here? I knew from Step Nine.

"You used to beat the crap out of me."

He nodded, then looked at his hands. He began flexing his fingers—sense memory of his ambushes? Down in front, Robin was introducing a singer, but we weren't listening.

"I was a violent person, Roger. I'm not that person anymore. And I am truly sorry for all the things I did to you."

It was my line, but I wasn't going to forgive him. I wasn't going to ask him to explain his violence. I didn't want to hear how he had become a man of peace via Jesus or Buddha. Nor was I going to ask him, "Why did you pick me?" Doing so would be as naked as karaoke. A target is a target is a target. I drained my glass, pulled my coat up from the floor. "Goodbye, Matt."

"Why are you going?"

"I don't do karaoke." It was the easiest thing to say.

"You don't?"

"Never have."

"Never ever?

"Not even once."

"You're really missing out."

"So be it," I snapped. "So. Matt. Matt Pedrick. It's been...."

"Real." He said it, not me. Very seventies.

We both stood. I did not extend my hand. Then—a revelation to make my knees wobble, one I could actually articulate—"I'm taller than you are."

He smiled. "Guess what, Roger?"

"What?" I said, swallowing hard.

"You always were."

While I processed that, he asked me whether we could have breakfast or lunch the next day. I lied and said that my flight left at five a.m. He asked if he could drive me to the airport, but I said I had a rental. He looked so downcast, I said that if the Morningwood Bar at the other end of the club were still open, he could buy me a proper cocktail, when I really wanted to say, "We're done here, Matt. Really and truly and forever done."

"I have to stay put," he said.

"Here?" I cocked an eyebrow.

"I have to hear Tacey."

"One of your children?" I guessed.

"My eldest," he said. "I'd like you to meet Tacey."

"Maybe next time," I said. I stood, then, planning my escape from the packed space, started to slide along the back wall. Matt stood too. He reached for my arm, but only got a handful of the coat I'd put between us. He could have my coat, if it came to that.

Robin announced, "Next up is Tacey Pedrick."

There were some whoops. Matt froze, but I kept moving, adding distance between us. A broad-shouldered, flat-chested blonde in a little black dress slunk into the spotlight and began a spiel. The better breed of karaoke singers, it turns out, polish their patter.

"This song is for my father," began Tacey. "He's in the house tonight. How great is that?" Polite applause. "So. When I was little, my father told me that he loved this song so much, he bought the 45 when it came out."

Tacey sipped some water. There was something to Tacey that reminded me of my most bad-ass Haverford students.

"I had to look that up," said Tacey. "Because, at first, I thought he meant a Colt 45."

The reference, easier to parse than "'zounds," drew some chuckles from the older patrons.

"Well, guess what? A 45 is a *record*. That you play on a *turntable*. My dad said he took a lot of shit in 1977 when the football team found that 45 in his gym bag. Do you want to know why? Because Linda Ronstadt sang it. Not Blue Oyster Cult. Or Led Zeppelin. Or RKO Speedwagon, whoever all the fuck they were." More laughter, some scattered boos. "But a girl. My dad loved a *girl* song, so the 1977 North Platte High School football team had a problem with it, can you imagine?"

Tacey bumped a hip. "Men."

"Damn straight," called out a man, but in a good-natured way.

"Damn straights is more like it," said Tacey, to a big laugh. "A weird-looking dude named Roy Orbison wrote this song, and recorded it first, in 1963, but to this day my dad and I think that Linda Ronstadt *owns* this song."

In the applause, Tacey nodded to Robin, who started the machine.

During the intro to, yes, "Blue Bayou," Matt caught up to me and grabbed my right arm. He repeated that Tacey was his eldest child. Their dead name was Theodore, after a Pedrick uncle who had been shot down in a helicopter in Vietnam.

"They're doing hormones," Matt said, unnecessarily, since Tacey's voice landed somewhere between Orbison and Ronstadt. "Tacey's mother can't deal with the situation. We've just separated. I've been living at the Ramada."

He was sweating, and didn't know where to look—at his child, at me, at the floor.

"They look like you, Matt."

"Really?"

"They have your build." I corrected myself. "Your old build."

"I tried to make them play football." Here, he shaded his eyes, as if he didn't want me to see him cry.

Obviously, I couldn't leave until they finished singing. In the applause, Matt turned to me and said, "Okay, we're up!"

"Up?"

"You and me."

No, we weren't. "We certainly are not."

"I want to sing with you, Roger. Come on."

"No."

"Please?"

"NO!"

Matt began pulling at my hands. I dropped my coat to get free, snagged my sweater along more of the wall, and made a break between two tables. He followed, like we were back in the high school lunchroom. I began shouting, "Get away from me, you can't make me!" (Sense memory, they call it.)

The crowd, thinking a fight was breaking out, was growing silent.

"What's going on back there?" said Robin.

"Nothing," Matt called out. "Just a friendly disagreement," he said, just as he had to the snickering hallway monitors, some of them teachers, some of them parents.

"Now you behave, fellas," said Robin.

I'd put another table between us. The door was maybe twenty feet away.

"Sister Essence, it's me," shouted Matt, as if calling on a superhero.

"Hey, everybody, meet Tacey's father, my radiologist, Dr. Matthew Pedrick."

"R is for Radiologist," quoted someone in the audience. "Bringer of bad news!"

"Can you keep Roger in here!" asked Matt. "I want to sing with him."

"Jolly Roger?" she said.

"Don't let him get away!"

"I sure won't." To block my exit, she began heading to the host station.

"Stop bullying me!" I said, way too loudly.

In the quiet, Tacey Pedrick, still on stage, said, "You heard the man, Dad." Their tone spoke to a lifetime of paternal pressures, but I thought I heard acceptance somewhere in there too. (I could have been imagining that.)

With the diminished dexterity of an ex-football player approaching retirement, Matt got down on his knees a table away from me and, as if the channel had switched to a reality show called *Say Yes to the Ring*, asked me to please sing with him.

"No."

"Please."

"No, I can't, Matt. I really can't."

"Can't, or won't?" he said—like straight men have since the beginning of time.

"Both."

Trying to stand, he nearly fell over, but managed to recover, with the help of an astonished Millennial. I sensed the crowd had begun siding with him.

"How do I—how can I say this?" pleaded Matt.

He was handsome. He had always been handsome, the way I had always been taller. I might have crushed on him in high school if he hadn't been a total dick. "I would be most honored if you would sing with me, Roger."

"I do, I said, like I was in the last act of a lost Chekhov play. "I mean, I will."

I took his outstretched hand to fresh cheers, but shrank from his attempt at a bro hug. Was karaoke always this lunatic? Making our way to the stage, to the chant of "Jolly, Jolly, Jolly," I asked him if he had a song in mind.

"Mockingbird," he answered, as if that were a given.

"You mean Carly Simon—"

"And James Taylor.' It was already cued up for me to sing with Tacey."

I stepped onto the stage. In the heat of the spotlight, I needed Robin's handkerchief, or a stack of bar napkins. Tacey handed me their microphone. I passed it to Matt as if it were on fire.

"I don't know the words," I lied.

"Just follow along, doofus," said Matt jokingly, pointing to the screen below. Sure enough, I saw the words *Mock—Yeah—King—Yeah—Bird—Yeah—Yeah—Yeah*. So literal, I thought, beginning to hyperventilate.

"You be James," he said, "I'll be Carly."

He'd taken the bigger part, but it was the girl's part. So be it. Robin hit play.

Of course, I knew the words. I had bought the 45 too, belted along with Carly and James in my queer little Day-Glo fortress once upon a time. I started by just speaking my lines, but Matt's steady hand kept squeezing my forearm. Hadn't Sister Essence declared that compassion was a pie with more than one piece to it? By the time Matt got to "And if that better way ain't so," the entire audience heard me sing along, as if my life depended on it—"I'll ride with the tide and go with the flow." You could hear me, all right.

Amulet

This last story takes place before self-compassion became a thing. A couple of years ago, rather than continue to jump through the ever-narrowing, flaming hoops of campus identity politics, I retired myself as a drama professor at Haverford College. My husband, Elihu Fowler, or E.F., recently retired after thirty years as a pediatric nurse practitioner at Jefferson Hospital in downtown Philadelphia. Statistically speaking, we are living out the last quarter of our lives. In a previous quarter, on a commune, E.F. fathered and caught his four children (*Mothers* deliver their babies today; doctors catch them. Point taken.), and we have three grandsons.

Like both of his parents, and my mother, E.F. has begun suffering from cognitive loss. A few weeks ago, he opened a new memoir written by a cloistered nun (his favorite subject) and thought the words were printed in Cyrillic. He slammed the book shut; it hasn't happened since. He has begun mixing the lids, the pots, and the bowls in the organized kitchen drawers. At the end of two dinner parties, he has said to me in front of our guests, "Shouldn't we be going home now?" (Both of us could drink less, BTW.) An initial CAT scan showed more than the average amount of expected brain shrinkage in a man of 67.

In exchange for getting his hearing tested—poor hearing accelerates cognitive loss—E.F. has said I have to do something about my right hip. This after a near-decade of stumping around like Captain Hook. I fantasize that the orthopedist, looking at my X-ray, will exclaim, "How have you been living for so long with this level of pain? Your ball joint looks as fuzzy as a dandelion puff!" If I can't test well, let me test heroically.

When we return next month from our first self-declared bucket list vacation, eight days crossing from Brooklyn to Southampton on the

Queen Mary 2, then a week of castle-hopping in Scotland, I will find a hip guy and, after wrangling for the last longest with Kaiser Permanente, E.F. will get a pair of hearing aids, and an MRI.

We'd be needing tuxedos for dinners on the QM2. Why bother, asked a couple of hetero friends, when Cunard has relaxed its dress code? Can you say *Now, Voyager*? Can you say *The Lady Eve*? Can you say *Gentlemen Prefer Blondes*? E.F. pulled his Brooks Brothers tux out from the back of the guest room closet. In a pants pocket, he found a ticket for a gala performance of *Madame Butterfly* at the Met, dated 2014. E.F. loves the opera; me, scarcely. Because of his penchant for nuns, his hands-down favorite is Poulenc's *Dialogues of the Carmelites.*

"Christ, that was forever ago," I said, referring to the ticket. "Have we not been in tuxes all these years?"

"Apparently not."

"We've clearly lost our luster. Do you remember the production?"

"Of course I do. The Ciao-Ciao San was Czech."

Asking E.F. whether he remembered specific details is going to become more and more of a fraught question as we tumble into the end zone. We've been praying he'll get into a trial study for Metformin, a diabetes drug with the potential to hoover up the brain plaque linked to Alzheimer's.

"The pants feel too tight in the waist."

That was E.F.'s way of saying he wanted a new tux.

"Let me try them on," I said. "If they fit me, we won't have to buy two." I had long busted out of the double-breasted vintage number that I wore whenever I could in my thirties and forties.

E.F.'s pants were snug on me too, and too short, but the waist and cuffs could be altered. I was reaching inside the suit bag to pull out the tux jacket when I spotted a white, hand-printed address tag in the ID holder.

Mr. Roger Hauf
Anantara Bangkok Sathorn Hotel
further#2702
Tel: --02210-9000

I dropped the bag and vocalized something near to a screech. I pointed to the tag. "Bangkok," I said, like Orson Welles croaking, "Rosebud."

"What's wrong, honey?"

"This is the bag that our suits came in the night before we flew home from Thailand. Remember? That's the address of our hotel. Were we really on the 27th floor? Oh God, remember the smell? The heat? How badly I behaved? I should have died, but I didn't."

I sat on the guest bed and covered my face with my hands. Certain shames can never be vanquished.

"No, you didn't die," said E.F. "You're not allowed to die."

He sat beside me and stroked the back of my neck. He remembered.

"Oh God, E.F., I promise to be good on this trip."

"Of course you will."

"I'm not the same person I was in Thailand."

"You're not, Roger, absolutely not."

"Are you sure?" I sure wasn't sure. Does the core of a person ever actually change?

"And neither am I," he said, wryly acknowledging the changes to his brain.

In the summer of 2012, we traveled to Thailand to celebrate the 50th birthday of Shreve Wilmary, the brother of a close colleague of E.F.'s at Jefferson. Shreve was a Harvard-trained internist who lived in Bangkok, where he owned and operated a male brothel (!). From the size of his passport, three times as thick with stamps and visas as that of a regular American, Shreve had to be a CIA operative. Brothelkeeper struck me then—and does still—as a genius occupational cover for a life of espionage.

There were twelve on the trip, including three Wilmary children whose interests monopolized their parents' schedules. That left E.F. and me to our own sightseeing for the four days we'd be in the capital. On our first morning we did what one does first: tour the Wat Phra Kaew

(Grand Palace complex) to see the Emerald Buddha, and then on to the nearby Wat Pho, the temple that houses the famous Reclining Buddha.

Navigating megacities is work. Our hotel in the Sathorn district was centrally located, but it still took us forty minutes to walk down St. Louis Road to get to the Saphan Taksin transportation hub. Then it took another twenty minutes before the next northbound Chao Praya riverboat turned up, then another half an hour on the boat, where I couldn't decide from the waterlogged map nailed to a life preserver whether to get off at Chang Pier or Maharaj Pier. A smartphone would have resolved this travel crux, but we didn't have them then.

I chose Maharaj, and in no time, we'd reached the wall enclosing the Wat Phra Kaew, a compound whose total acreage is *one-third* the size of New York's Central Park. Reaching did not mean breaching; there was no signage indicating where breaks in the wall offered ingress. All that was visible from the street were dozens of *non-dòp*, glittering spires topping the dozens of temples inside. Very *King and I*, if you know that Rodgers and Hammerstein classic, in bad odor nowadays for its glorification of the British Empire and its infantilization of the Siamese people.

The passengers who had disembarked with us had somehow vanished. We saw no savvy tourists to trail. E.F. and I traveled southward along the wall a great distance, then turned the corner and headed east for twenty minutes. Still no way in. Before we reached the southeast corner of the compound on Khao San Road, we'd begun bickering in the ninety-two-degree heat about who had left *Fodor's Thailand* in our hotel room. My long-sleeved shirt and long pants (*de rigueur* for temple visits), my bandana neckerchief, and leather fanny pack were all sticking to my body. My feet already hurt. My eyelids were sweating. Moisture pearled in the crooks of my fingers. My face, normally the color of a deli package of Danish ham, was getting even pinker. I was radiating bad energy.

A Thai man in a suit approached us and bowed with folded prayer hands touching his chin. "*Sawatdee khrap,*" he said, then asked if we needed assistance.

E.F. returned the traditional *sawatdee khrap*. I cut to the chase. "We want to see the Wat Phra Kaew," I said, hoping to score points by using its Thai name.

"Ah, of course."

I waved my hand at the wall, stretching north for blocks. "We can't find an entrance. Where do we get in?"

He ignored the question and said, "I am sorry to say, Sir, that the Grand Palace is closed for lunch from twelve to two this afternoon."

"It is?"

The assertion was so fishy, so outrageous that the longer the man held his poker face, the more it might be true. How would we know? Shreve Wilmary had warned us at breakfast of Thailand's *lèse majesté* laws, almost the strictest in the world. If we made audible fun of King Bhumibol, or any member of the royal family, we were looking at fifteen years in prison. Seriously. A country with that level of civil control could very well shut the gates of its government for lunch.

"There are many other wonderful sights to see while you wait for the palace to reopen."

E.F. nodded. The man flicked his hand, and instantly, a *tuk-tuk* rolled up, jingling like a Good Humor truck.

Tuk-tuks are motorized rickshaws designed to get through traffic jams. There are thousands of them in the streets of Bangkok, each a hand-wrought carnival of charms, bells, pom-poms, and icons that synchs with the aesthetic fantasies and beliefs of its driver. There are all-Elvis *tuk-tuks*, Manchester United *tuk-tuks*, Hello Kitty *tuk-tuks*—everything and everyone, I expect, except Henry Kissinger, roasting down below between Pol Pot and Antonin Scalia. Like Venetians and their gondolas, the Thai people eschew *tuk-tuks* for taxis, but tourists will and do take them, despite the noise, the pollution, and an inability to see anything above their low canopies.

The man and the driver, who looked all of thirteen, began a conversation in their language. I started to get a terrible feeling. Remember how Pee-Wee Herman discovers at the end of his *Big Adventure* that there is no basement in the Alamo? When Molière famously wrote that human beings can endure everything except ridicule, he had me in mind.

"What time is it?" I asked.

"Almost one," said E.F. "You can't take another hour in this heat, Rog."

"Then let's get lunch somewhere."

"We had that huge breakfast buffet not two hours ago."

"Fine. Then let's have a vendor cut open some coconuts for us, and we can sit and drink them in the shade."

"Do you see any street vendors? Or shade?" said E.F., pointing to the treeless, six-lane business artery beside us.

The man turned back. "You like silks? Jewels? Amulets?

"NO," I lied, with such force that E.F. laughed. Who doesn't want his own ruby or emerald or yards of silk as saffron as a goldfinch, or as scarlet as a peony? Like all First Worlders, we were also in Bangkok to shop. We'd be ordering bespoke suits and shirts with Shreve's tailor before we left for Chang Mai in four days, and having them delivered the night before we flew home. Thai massages had been scheduled, and we'd visit the Jim Thompson House, and E.F. was going to take a course at the famous Blue Elephant Cooking School.

I started moving away from the *tuk-tuk*. "Let's go, E.F. There is no way that the entire Grand Palace compound is closed for lunch," but E.F. shot me a rare "Don't be a dick" look.

I am a disaster with foreign beggars, shills, and touts. My tenth circle of hell, after Burning Man on a bottomless bowl of butternut squash, would be getting dropped into a Moroccan or a Turkish souk. Not so my husband: when E.F. refuses the little boy asking him whether he wants to see the giant tortoises on Prisoner Island, the tout hears a clear, firm but polite 'no,' and moves on. When I say 'no,' the boy smells a potential 'yes' deep underneath and persists until my 'nos' get louder and more embarrassing. Confronted by a crowd of the needy, I am so afraid of being taken for a ride, and so overwhelmed by my inability to satisfy them all, I want to lay down in the dust and say, "Take all of my money and then eat my body like Sebastian Venable in *Suddenly Last Summer*." E.F. insists that the touts don't take refusals personally. He says, "They're just doing their job"—a line I play back to him whenever he marvels at how actors learn all those lines.

Bangkok touts weren't so obvious. We were taken for a ride, price negotiated in advance. E.F. got in first. I hesitated, then, acting upon the insane notion that I could report him to the police if we were robbed and then thrown into the Chao Raya, I asked the man for his name.

He smiled. Facial movement at last. "Fred."

"Fred what?"

"Fred Sambandaraksa." (Some names you never forget.)

The plastic seats in the *tuk-tuk* were a fresh adhesive to my sweltering habitus, and the fumes generated by all the cars whizzing around us were insufferable. The driver had no English. Where we were headed was a mystery, but I did know that the royal compound was receding in the distance. We'd randomly stop, where Fred-like salesmen, waggling bottles of water in the doorways of their shops bearing "AIR-CONDITIONED" signage, waved us inside. E.F. would go in with the driver, but I seethed on principle in the *tuk-tuk*. My bad energy could have set the canopy fringe on fire.

A purchase would have made E.F. a traitor in my eyes, so he knew to come back empty-handed. At 1:45, I thrust his left arm forward in the tuk-tuk to the driver's left, and pointed to his watch. "Take us back to the palace. Now."

Once inside the complex, how could the magnificent, multilayered *otherness* of Thai culture fail to improve my mood? I was agog. I was thrown back to grade school, when the marvels of the world unfolded day by day in social studies class, when the countries on the globe atop my dresser were as magically hued as the faces and uniforms on the thirty-foot tall Yaksha, ogres from Hindu mythology who guarded the gates to the most important temples in the Wat Phra Kaew. The lack of visual reference to Western ways and means, not to mention Jesus and the Greatest Story Ever Told, was thrilling. (The fantastical gilt creatures and deities and ziggurat-like structures had more in common—in a positive way—with *Minecraft* and the *Transformers* figures our grandson Tex is obsessed with.)

Before entering the Temple of the Emerald Buddha, we studied the nearly two hundred *Ramakien* mural panels in the Phra Rabian Gallery, a cloister that surrounds the temple. A creation myth for the country, and the source for two forms of classical Thai theater, the *Ramakien* is the Thai mutation of the Indian epic *Ramayana*. Its central narrative is the love of Phra Ram and Nang Sida, who is abducted by Ravana, the evil, ten-faced, twenty-armed King of Lanka, and rescued with the aid of Hanuman, the mischievous, but ultimately righteous monkey god.

You know how the Venus of Willendorf, the Paleolithic goddess figurine key to the history of Western Art, is only 4.4 inches tall? So it is with the seated Emerald Buddha, the palladium of Thailand. Made of jasper or jade—he is too sacred to undergo compositional analysis—he is but slightly over two feet tall. I loved that the King himself changed the little Buddha's golden robe three times a year in a public ceremony to match the summer, rainy, and cool seasons.

In a dimensional contrast that Lewis Carroll would have envied, the gold-leafed Reclining Buddha in the Wat Pho, across the street from the palace wall, was 151 feet long and fifty feet tall. After circling his immensity, one sits or lays down on mats in reverence. It is forbidden to show your feet to a Buddha; when facing him, you must sit on them or tuck them behind you. A couple hundred of us silently lined our footwear by the entrance to contemplate the vastness of the Buddha as he, resting his head on his raised left palm, contemplated, and to my mind, protected us from all harm. In those moments with him, I experienced an all-too-rare feeling of floating gently in the slipstream of time. It was hard to collect my shoes and leave, especially when I knew that we would never see him again.

On the return boat to the Saphin Takson, I reviewed the *tuk-tuk* drama and came to understand the scheme. Fred Sambandaraksa paid our driver to travel a certain circuit of shops every day. The shop owners recorded the number of *tuk-tuks* who showed up with tourists, and gave a commission to Fred, who then gave a cut to the driver, the lowest tout on the ladder. It didn't matter whether the passengers made any purchases, although sales would obviously up everyone's take.

E.F. can fall asleep anywhere, even in a riverboat packed with commuters. I nudged him awake on our bench and asked him how much he had paid the *tuk-tuk* driver.

"Eighty *baht*."

"How much is that in dollars?"

He hesitated. He knew I knew what he was thinking.

"No, tell me."

"About $1.75," he said, lifting an eyebrow in a rare gesture of reproval.

"Oh, Jesus."

"Mmmm," he said.

I felt wretched. The unequal distribution of wealth was the enemy, not the kid just doing his job, and I'd been a complete and utter asshole to begrudge him the miniscule fare. I sat quietly in the stink of myself until we reached the edge of our hotel, where there was another odor that I had already taken in that morning. In the air surrounding an enormous support column in the macadam drop-off to the lobby was a smell, not overly pungent, of dead goldfish in a bowl.

I took it in again. "Can you smell that?"

E.F. stopped and sniffed. "I don't smell anything."

"You don't?"

I can't say this was a surprise. I smell the carton of milk turning two days before E.F. can, and along with our cats, I know when a mouse has died behind the cabinets.

"What does it smell like?"

"Fish sauce, or sewage. Or rotting marsh plants in September."

We stood for a moment. A black town car was disgorging a pair of Chinese women in Jackie O sunglasses and dazzling, gold-threaded *cheongsams*. In the lobby, among tall, iron sculptures of stylized candle flames, a uniformed waiter proffered glasses of iced lemon water to the seated guests waiting to be checked in.

"I really don't smell anything," said E.F.

"I'm not imagining it."

"I know, Rog, I know."

✳

The next day, at the breakfast buffet on the second floor, we set coffee cups at Shreve Wilmary's table, then set out for sustenance. Every possible global foodstuff was artfully arranged in a room that sat four hundred: *Schinken* and cheese for the Germans; congee for the Asians; baked beans, blood sausage, kippers, mushrooms, and tomatoes for the Brits and Irish; bacon, eggs, three kinds of sausage, hash browns and home fries and grits, pancakes, waffles, French toast, and biscuits for the Americans. Lox and gravlax and sable and smelts and prawns and oysters and whitefish salad. Pierogi. Won-tons. Sushi. Seven kinds of juice. Espresso and cappuccino and Turkish coffee machines. A yogurt and cereal and granola bar with nuts, berries, and fruits, the familiar and the exotic. Doughnuts, pastries, baguettes, cookies, ice creams, sorbets. Nutella, marmite, peanut butter. There was an omelet station and a burrito station, a *bahn mi* station, and a Crèpes Suzette station.

For the Hauf family, "All You Can Eat" means "Eat All You Can," but that morning I had commitment issues with my plate—which means I wasn't really hungry. So I drifted, listening to the squeals of pleasure as patrons marveled to find all their hometown favorites. It was as if the giant Reclining Buddha had gotten up to whisk away the ceiling to shower our coop with handfuls of ambrosial chicken feed.

I fell in line behind E.F. at the omelet station. In accord with the rubric of plenty, there were fifteen ingredients in three rows of copper bowls between the two chefs.

"I just don't know what I want to eat," I sighed.

"Should I check for a fever?" said E.F.

"Funny. Too much choice."

"You didn't have this problem yesterday."

E.F. placed his order: sausage and green peppers. The chef on the left poured the egg slurry into the *sautier*; the chef on the right nodded to me.

"*Sawatdee khrap*," I said. "Ham and cheese, please."

"No mushrooms?" said E.F.

"Too much choice."

From under a bulb warmer beside him, the chef lifted a plate with a pre-made omelet and offered it to me. "Ham and cheese," he said.

I don't know what came over me in this moment; perhaps the Demon of Heinous White Privilege—let's call her Karen—persuaded the evil King Ravana to invade my being, because I refused the outstretched plate with all twenty of my arms, snapped, "I want my own omelet," and stomped away.

I poured myself some coffee and sat with Shreve, who was finishing a newspaper. His plate held passion fruit halves emptied of their custard.

"No breakfast?" said Shreve.

"I'm not hungry."

I'd been wanting to ask Shreve the whys and wherefores of running a male cathouse but this wasn't the moment, since his nieces and nephew, unaware of his day job, might turn up at the table. While showing E.F. and me the website for his establishment, *Preppy Lotus Lads,* (blocked by U.S. servers), Shreve was emphatic that his "boys"— eighteen to twenty-three, although they would playact any age for their johns—got tested weekly for disease, and that they earned roughly twenty times as much as they would back in their villages, if such a thing as jobs existed there. They sent most of their earnings home to their families. Shreve emphasized he was not a trafficker; he was offering his lads a certain amount of agency. Recalling all the sex I'd given away for free in my twenties, this seemed a reasonable exchange at the time. Today, I don't know where I would stand on the issue. The older you get, the grayer things become.

E.F. set down his omelet and a glass of watermelon juice. His not looking at me meant he disapproved of what had just gone down at the omelet station. I wish the opposite were possible, but E.F. never behaves badly, and I just have to live with that.

Referencing the newspaper, E.F. asked Shreve what was the latest with King Bhumibol.

Cutting in, I defied the edict against *lèse majesté* and said that King Bhumibol had been diagnosed with tertiary syphilis. Shreve told me in a serious tone to disguise his name at the very least.

"King Roomyball has syphilis."

"Ixnay on the Ingkay."

"Roomyballs has syphilis."

"Roomyball*bag,*" said Shreve. I laughed.

"Roomynutsack," I said.

"*Lumpy*nutsack," said Shreve, laughing too. "But let's Thai it up."

"How do you mean?"

"Add 'prikpoon.' Or 'prikporn' or 'longkorn.'"

"Like Prince Chulalongkorn, the snotty oldest son in *The King and I.*"

"Etcetera etcetera etcetera," said Shreve, in his best Yul Brynner.

"When I kneel, you shall kneel," I said in my best Yul Brynner.

"Did you know that 'We Kiss in a Shadow' was a secret gay anthem in the 1950s?"

I quoted Hammerstein: "'Our evenings are free and over too soon.'"

Shreve started up again. "Lumpyprickpoonnutsack."

"Lumpylungkornprikpornnutsack!"

Making fun of foreign names? Can you say 'racist'? Can you say *South Park*? Can you say 'laugh whores'? Shreve and I might have kept it up and brought Queen Sikrit ('Sicktits' springs first to mind) to the party, but E.F., silent during this game of Ugly American scrotal volleyball, was pointing me out to somebody. We couldn't have been louder than the breakfast din, so I squelched the thought that I was about to be arrested, then turned in my seat to see who E.F. saw.

The omelet chef had found me in the crowded restaurant. He set a plate in front of me, bowed, meekly said, "Ham and cheese, Sir" and slipped away to his station.

Made to order.

Eating crow doesn't cover what I felt as I forced it down. Shreve, hearing the story from E.F., said that Thais will go to extreme lengths to avoid causing displeasure in others. Refusing the initial pre-made omelet had, in fact, shamed the chef.

The years had covered over this wretched incident until Mr. Roger Hauf/Anantara Bangkok Sathorn Hotel reappeared on a black plastic suit bag in our guest room closet. At the time, I could have followed the chef back to the omelet station and begged his forgiveness. I could have given him 500 *baht* or 1000 *baht* to repair the damage, but shame carries no price tag. Post-breakfast in Room 2702, I had a complete come-apart. I sobbed. I pounded the bed with my fists, kicked with my feet. I'd cling to E.F., then push him away. I'd tear open the drapes and consider a leap. Why was I such an awful, horrible, terrible, miserable person? I hadn't been raised that way. How could E.F. stand me, put up with me for more than a week, I deserved to be alone, why wasn't I dead, I had deserved to die of AIDS decades ago, I deserved to die right now and burn in hell, or come back in the next life as a *tuk-tuk* driver, or a boy selling twist-tied bags of cashews on the riverboat, why had I never gotten my richly deserved comeuppance, why had life given me everything when I gave back nothing yet always wanted more more more, how could I be so selfish and shitty and superior and sick, I was the stink outside the lobby I was the rotting fish I was the rot...

Then, at some point during my mad scene, I noticed an opal and gold elephant amulet out on E.F.'s dresser, next to his change and our room keycard.

"What is this?" I screamed.

"It's an amulet," he said.

"I know it's a fucking amulet! I want to know where you bought it!"

"In one of the shops the *tuk-tuk* took us to."

Of course he would do that. Of course he would play along. Of course he would never deliberately offend someone. Amulets offer protection. E.F. had bought the amulet as protection from me. I flung it at him, then myself onto the bed, my face wet with tears and snot.

"Why are you so fucking goddam *good*, E.F.? Sometimes your goodness makes me sick."

(In Fugard's *A Lesson From Aloes,* Gladys says to her husband, Piet, that his goodness has become a terrible provocation.)

He lay down next to me and placed a hand in the center of my back. "I can only be who I am, Roger."

When I was finally able to pull it together, we left the hotel, this time with *Lonely Planet,* this time in shorts and polo shirts—no temples today—and strolled up Si Lon Road. I would be lying if I said that the temperature had dropped twenty degrees, that there was a lovely breeze, that smiling children decorated me with flower necklaces, and that a Bengal tiger held up its paw for me to hold, but I did feel better.

We spotted a sidewalk barber. Getting shaved is a luxury in the United States that involves insurance waivers and more instruments than a dental hygienist's tray, but here it cost about forty cents. E.F. likes to be shaved, and I liked the idea of doing something offbeat and non-touristy.

E.F. went first, and from his beatific expression, I could tell he was lost in the lather. My turn took five times as long. Eventually, I felt the barber marking my neck and chin with something. Was that a styptic pencil? That meant I was bleeding. Bleeding *en plein air* in Bangkok? How clean was the barber's razor? How many tropically diseased necks had he already nicked that day with his cesspool of pathogens? Was he transmitting a new, drug-resistant strain of HIV? Hadn't I just called to the heavens that I deserved to die?

Turns out that karma, in the form of Hanuman, the mischievous monkey king had, by making the barber draw my blood in seven different spots, intervened to pay me back for shaming the omelet chef. It made me feel even better.

Years later, reading about megacities, I learned the source of that odor too faint for E.F.'s nose: Bangkok is crisscrossed by a network of artificial canals. Our hotel steeped in brackish water. The average daily summer temperature there is in the mid-nineties. Heat plus standing water plus the urban run-off of eleven million people equals feculence. Although not built on canals, 18th century Philadelphia was similar to Old Bangkok, especially during yellow fever season, when the high and well-connected could repair to the country for fresh air and safety.

We sail next week on the Queen Mary. E.F. is a kid at Christmas, and I'm a fifth-grader on a Friday afternoon with no homework. Yesterday, I brought E.F.'s altered tux back from Baldwin's downtown. Afterwards, in a bookstore, I picked up the most recent *Fodor's Essential Thailand* and (re)learned that the Thai are among the kindest, gentlest people on earth. Moreover, the Wat Phra Kaew is open from 8:30 a.m. to 3:30 p.m. every day—and finally this, in connection to the Jim Thompson House—one was to beware of "well-dressed touts who will tell you that the house is closed and try to haul you off on a dodgy buying spree."

Tonight, we got into harness together. Tuxedos are contraptions, to say the least, but so worth the effort, even down to the pesky bow ties. We hooked each other's cummerbunds and put in each other's cufflinks.

E.F., for once playing the peacock, had gone a little crazy and bought ruby shirt studs and a pair of scarlet velvet slippers. He laughed when I told him he looked hot.

"You look great too," he said.

"Borrowed glory, sweetheart," I said, 'Borrowed glory. This was your tux first." I wanted to tell him that, in the fitting the day before, while the tailor clipped runaway threads, I had wished it were possible to absorb even a smidgen of his goodness through the fabric of his made-over formal wear.

"We have to take a picture for the kids," I said. "We'll forget once we're on board."

"A positively ripping idea," said E.F., adopting a British accent.

We positioned ourselves in front of the wall of books. I held the camera. Between flashes, I thought of King Bhumibol changing the Emerald Buddha three times a year. Did the little Buddha have a favorite golden robe? Did he look forward most to summer, rainy, or cool?

"We'll be on the high seas for Father's Day," I said.

"Topping. Ought we send telegrams to the offspring?"

"Capital. So much posher than a vile text," I said, playing along.

We hung up the tuxedos, sent a photo to the family that we could agree on, decided on which suitcases to take and what kind of alcohol to bring (Cunard permits just one bottle per passenger), and remembered that we were going to have to score some Avon Skin-So-Soft to repel Scotland's famous midges. Not that we were planning to take any long outdoor hikes with my bum hip.

The cats, who know when we're taking a trip, came into the guest room. Nash, already sulking about it, hopped into his cardboard box on the radiator. His brother, Wally, bleated and jumped onto the bed to demand another dose of affection. We love these boys so much that we joke that they can't die before us.

"What's for dinner?" asked E.F.

For an instant, I froze. E.F. heard an exhalation, I hope, instead of my pained sigh. I was going to have to get better at this. With as much calm as I could muster, I reminded him that we had already eaten dinner. "I made *picadillo*, remember? And a carrot slaw."

"Right."

"If you're still hungry, we could have dessert. There are Klondike bars in the freezer."

His smile was rueful. "I'm sorry, Rog."

"I know," I said, preparing.

About the Author

James Magruder has published four other books of fiction: *Sugarless, Let Me See It, Love Slaves of Helen Hadley Hall*, and *Vamp Until Ready* (also from Rattling Good Yarns). Yale University Press published his *Three French Comedies*, a collection of translations that was cited as an "Outstanding Literary Translation of the Year" by the American Literary Translators Association; and *The Play's the Thing: Fifty Years of Yale Repertory Theatre (1966-2016)*, his first—and last—book of non-fiction. His translations and adaptations of works by Marivaux, Molière, Lesage, Labiche, Gozzi, Dancourt, Hofmannsthal, Dickens, and Giraudoux have been produced off-Broadway, across the country, and in England, Japan, Australia, and Germany. He wrote, or co-wrote, the books for two Broadway musicals, *Triumph of Love*, and the more recent *Head Over Heels*, a deeply queer, blank verse mashup of Sir Philip Sidney's *Arcadia* (1590) and the song catalog of the Go-Go's. He is a five-time MacDowell Fellow and a 34-year resident of Baltimore.

Acknowledgements

Behind these stories are people, living and deceased, who have shaped and enriched my life in ways they never could have imagined: Lawrence Staib, Conrad Lesnewski, John Kunat, Eva Kaufman, Kate Makuen, Michael Brady, Barry Davis, Michael Slade, Richard Pickens, Matt Stockert, Catherine Weidner, Julia Reidhead, and David Nolta.

As ever, I'd like to thank my Baltimore writing cohort: Jane Delury, Christine Grillo, Kathy Flann, Elisabeth Dahl, Betsy Boyd, Marion Winik, and Liz Hazen.

I'd like to express my gratitude to Carla Zackson, Cornell Class of 1982, for the kind use of her photographic still.

Many thanks--again--to the patient and editorially scrupulous Ian Henzel, who, with Rattling Good Yarns Press, has created an ever-growing home for queer fiction and non-fiction writers.

As for my husband, Steve Bolton, *tout cela va sans dire*.